A former London Police Detective and regular panellist on BBC2's BAFTA winning TV series 'Ranganation', Cliff Kemp now lives in Buckinghamshire with his wife and two relentlessly growing children. He has previously written for local press on sports events and online for sports websites. He describes the writing of this novel as being one of the few things keeping him sane during the Pandemic and another thing Covid-19 has to answer for.

For Hannah, Isabel and Ethan. X

Cliff Kemp

LIVE. LIVE. REPEAT

AUSTIN MACAULEY PUBLISHERS™

LONDON · CAMBRIDGE · NEW YORK · SHARJAH

A CIP catalogue record for this title is available from the British Library.

ISBN 9781398437180 (Paperback)
ISBN 9781398437197 (ePub e-book)

www.austinmacauley.com

First Published 2022
Austin Macauley Publishers Ltd®
1 Canada Square
Canary Wharf
London
E14 5AA

Thanks to everyone who took the time to read all, or part of this, I know you all had better things to do. Thanks for saying enough nice things at the beginning to keep me typing. Thank you so much Hannah, for being brave enough to make me re-write the bits that only made sense in my head. And thanks to former Chancellor of the Exchequer, Mr. Rishi Sunak, whose furlough scheme ensured that I had no more excuses for not getting this thing written once and for all.

Your future is whatever you make it, so make it a good one.
– Doc Brown, *Back to the Future III*

Chapter 1

I'd been living in Spain for three years following the split with Nikki. We'd planned on moving out together, but while I was at work keeping on top of the Pound to Euro exchange rate, she was apparently keeping on top of Dave next door. I'd always had an inherent mistrust of people able to work from home effectively. This was mainly due to the fact that whenever given the opportunity myself, it had generally resulted in finishing an entire Netflix box set or some 'googling' that required an internet history delete.

Although Nikki had humoured me during discussions about emigrating, it was always more my dream than hers. I had a middle management job with a cardboard packaging manufacturer that I despised and a boss who I'd fantasised about murdering in so many different ways I was running out of imaginary things to push him off, things to hit him on the back of the head with and places around High Wycombe to hide his dismembered body. In fairness to him, I am sure he felt the same way about me; I clearly couldn't give a shit about my job, or the company, never really hid the fact, but never gave him quite enough reason to fire me. I'd catch him glaring at me across the office with a look reserved for someone you'd found trying to violate your Nan.

The final straw for me came when I was passed over for promotion by someone eminently more qualified, and deserving, and who would most certainly do a better job.

I was outraged.

Being the pro-level passive-aggressive I am, I wrote a sarcastic and strongly worded resignation email (timed to send once I'd slipped out the door like the coward I am), never to return. I did this at 10:03 a.m. on Tuesday. Evidently leaving the office early was more of a surprise to Nikki that day than it will have been to my boss Bill. Returning home, my feeling of relief and exhilaration was replaced by one of confusion at seeing Dave from next door come walking out of my bathroom stark bollock naked with my 'World's Best Husband' mug clasped in a soapy hand.

I think I might have said 'right then' or something equally lame and British as we stood in my hallway with him dripping water all over my laminate flooring. His mouth flapped up and down a bit but not in any way that would formulate actual coherent words. I think my first thought was 'screw you then Dave, you're not having your hedge trimmer back'.

The next 30 seconds or so is a bit of a blur but I certainly swung something like a punch but at about the same time that Nikki came bundling out of the bathroom with a towel dragged hastily around her. This resulted in my, less than Mike Tyson like, blow being absorbed mainly by Nikki's towel which sent her backwards into Dave, her legs sliding across at me sending all of us sprawling on the wet landing. By the time the indistinguishable chaos of arms, legs and genitals had separated into three separate humans again, the fight had gone out of me. My desire to wreak a terrible revenge on them both was outweighed by my desire to not accidentally touch Dave's knob.

Although Nikki and I had been together since our mid-twenties, having met one starry night outside KFC in Hemel Hempstead, we had never been bothered about having kids. My reasons had been predominantly financial where hers were always about the physical effects on her. I specifically remember Nikki saying in response to a friend who had recently experienced the miracle of childbirth that she 'didn't want to…', and I think I recall this profound moment correctly, '…end up with a lady garden like a punched lasagne'. I haven't been able to eat Italian food since.

I had nothing to keep me in England. No wife, kids, or job, my dad has passed the year before after a cruel illness that left him a shell of the man I'd previously known, and I lost my mum in a bizarre accident in my teens. She had been my world and my best mate. I had plenty of other mates, don't get me wrong, it wasn't a Norman Bates situation, but we were super close, could always make each other laugh, and she was perfect in every way.

Sure, time blurs the imperfections, but I don't really ever remember being truly happy after she died. One ordinary Tuesday, Mum was standing on a train platform on her way to meet some friends in London for a girlie shopping trip when a guy came bundling past her being chased by the local Old Bill. The guy tripped over the strap of the bag he'd stolen and pushed Mum onto the tracks as the 10:34 from Birmingham New Street was flying through the station. She'd have known very little about it.

Mum loved Spain and our family holidays from when I was a kid hold almost all of my happiest memories. It was another reason to pack up and move there.

I rented an apartment in a little town called Roquetas de Mar which sat on the Costa Del Sol, a nice balance of friendly locals and ex-pats but far enough from Malaga and Marbella to avoid being too close to lots of what I was trying to get away from. My apartment was less than luxurious but, if you stood with one foot on the sofa and the other on the flip-top bin, on a very clear day, on tip-toes, you could almost make out the Mediterranean Sea. My Paradise.

About three weeks into my adventure and wondering what I was going to do once the savings had run out, I got to talk to a guy in a bar. As one is tended to do. He was returning to the UK having very deliberately blown all his savings on beer and prostitutes, purely to prevent his ex-wife from getting her hands on any of it. He had been operating a small pool cleaning business amongst the ex-pat community and was simply going to let it fizzle out.

I bought the list of clients, some dangerous-looking chemicals and a couple of nets from him for the price of two pints of Guinness and a packet of prawn cocktail crisps. I began to imagine my Pool cleaning empire, managed to expand the business further and even hired myself an employee when demand quickly outstripped my work ethic.

Juan had all the core skills required to be a highly successful pool cleaner. He was never more than an hour and a half late for work and looked good with his shirt off. He was almost certainly providing 'extra services' to at least four of the communities golf widows. I realised he was still 'visiting' one of these ladies (and that we were still collecting the direct debit) six months after they'd had their pool filled in and turned into a tennis court.

Even after 18 months of working together, he would still smile graciously when I would call after him with a jolly, "See you at 'Juan' o'clock!" in an exaggerated Spanish accent.

He almost certainly hated me, and without doubt, thought I was a little bit racist.

I'd turned up in the Costa del Sol with what was left of the proceeds of the house sale and schoolboy Spanish. I was able to ask where the library was, what time the bus to Madrid left as well as explain to people that I liked playing football with my friends on Saturdays. At 38 years, I was still in reasonable shape and not a bad looking guy, but it quickly became apparent that the local females weren't going to be charmed into bed by being asked if the bakery was open on Wednesdays.

I eventually managed to pick up enough 'Spanglish' to get by (most of the locals spoke better English than I did), had become a frustratingly poor golfer and made enough money to drink myself into oblivion every night at 'Churchill's'.

Living the dream.

'Churchill's' was your stereotypical British bar frequented predominantly by retired Black Cab drivers, over-the-hill gangster wannabes and a cocktail of people running away from something... although for the main part, that was the British weather. Anyone under 68 years old was automatically called 'Young man' by everyone else in there.

A signed photo of Ray Winston with Gary, the owner, took pride of place above the bar. TV screens showing Premier League football matches hung from every available piece of wall space not taken up by pictures of the Queen or dogs playing snooker.

Julie, Mrs Gary, served behind the bar what seemed to be 24 hours a day, seven days a week. I don't think I ever went in, and she wasn't stood there in her mini-skirt and boob tube two sizes too small. Despite this, the skin on her face was so tanned and lined it looked like a leather satchel that had been run over by a reasonably sized van. Twice.

Make-up must have been applied using some sort of heavy industrial machinery and despite being somewhere between 45 and 80 (it was impossible to tell with any greater level of accuracy), she still got plenty of attention from the dirty old bastards who would sit at the bar and deliberately make her bend over to reach the beers on the bottom shelf of the fridge. I'm not proud to say I'd even glanced at myself during leaner periods.

Life in Spain had settled into something akin to a crap holiday. Albeit one where you had to clean other people's swimming pools. Forced conversation with people you would never normally have anything to do with, sunburn, sweat and mosquito bites. Genuine contentedness was only really reached this time last year when I heard via an old friend that two weeks after getting engaged, Dave 'next door' had caught Nikki and his best mate playing tonsil tennis in a bar in Slough.

I regularly thought about returning to England's green and pleasant land's, but these musings never lasted long as I would soon remember how much I hated the bloody place. I made a list of what I disliked about England one time when I had seriously considered returning home.

This is the first page. I lost the other three:

rain
pets on social media
traffic lights
hoodies
the Royal Family
Asda
neighbours (not the TV program)
neighbours (the TV program)
cyclists
smart cars
Piers Morgan
London
Nikki
The M4
cycle lanes
bus lanes
country lanes
black pudding
clouds
wagon wheels

I took the longer route to the pub on this particular Friday evening to give myself time to remember my list. It hadn't been the best of days. I'd turned up at the Thomson's Villa with them still in bed recovering from one of their 'couples parties' the previous evening. This 'party' had clearly moved to the pool at some point during proceedings and the first part of my working day involved fishing an array of variously sized dildos from the bottom of their deep end.

Fortunately, not a euphemism. For my own amusement, I lined them up in size order along their breakfast bar before I left. With gloves on. That I threw away after. The day concluded with me chasing a deposit Mrs Myers granddaughter had generously left in the plunge pool, with my leaf net.

The longer route took me along about 500 yards of beachside promenade. As I began to make the turn from the seafront towards the bars, cafes and myriad gift shops, I stopped for a second longer than usual to take in the 'Med' in all its glory. "This is why I came," I thought.

I sighed, turned away and instantly found myself entangled in the lead of a ludicrously small, rat-like, dog that had appeared in my path. I stumbled and cursed as the owner, a ludicrously small, rat-like, Spanish woman, muttered something aggressively under her breath. Probably an apology.

I composed myself, slipped back into my flip flops and made my way to the pub. Although I'd had better days, it was nothing six pints of San Miguel wasn't more than capable of dealing with.

Despite its many, *many* faults, you could walk into 'Churchill's' on any night and, other than the odd disappointed tourist, know everyone in there. Sometimes that's exactly what you needed. Same faces, same crap banter, same dirty old bastards at the bar leering at Julie, Crazy Brian watching porn on his phone in the corner whilst pretending to watch the news and Gary retelling the same story about how he hit one of the Krays with his Austin Healy once.

Same people. Same faces.

But not tonight.

Chapter 2

It was extremely rare to see a local in 'Churchill's'. They had their own tapas bars and 'chinguitas' that they frequented and the lure of watching Burnley v Watford on a Sunday afternoon or listening to Gary murder Elvis Presley daily on the Karaoke clearly didn't seem to do it for them.

I felt a subtle difference in the atmosphere the second I walked in. As usual, I looked up and down the bar to see if any of the regulars I didn't want to punch in the face, were in this evening. Unfortunately, for me, they weren't. I had the choice to either listen to smutty jokes I'd heard a thousand times at the bar or plump for option 2.

Option 2 was to grab the seat next to the swarthy looking fellow perched on a stool at the end of the bar. This was where Gary hung all his West Ham scarves and a picture of himself with Chas and Dave that he'd clearly photoshopped. After the day I'd had, I just couldn't face an evening of hilarity at the bar where the punchlines were all accompanied by lude hand gestures. Option 2 it was then.

The presence of the non-regular patron was causing some concern amongst the other customers who were doing all they could, and by that I mean whispering amongst themselves and scowling a bit, to make the man feel uncomfortable enough to bugger off. What if he wanted to join in with the quiz? What if he left the bar and sat down at the Johnsons table who were yet to arrive? What if he wasn't just tanned but was actually Spanish? I hadn't sensed this amount of unease in Churchill's since Julie's left nipple had made an impromptu appearance at last year's Boxing Day dinner.

As I made my way self-consciously to the only vacant stool at the bar, I felt like Richard Dreyfuss in Close Encounters. I could feel all eyes on me, burning into the back of my neck, angry and indignant at my betrayal.

'Alright?' I said to the guy as I sat and motioned to Gary for my usual.

The man was sat hunched over a shot glass of some clear liquid and made me wait an uncomfortable amount of time before responding.

'Senor' He replied without looking up from his glass.

Fuck. Spanish.

I glanced over my shoulder to the audience of narrowed eyes and shaking heads. 'We could have told you that' their expressions screamed at me. I pretended not to notice.

In my head, I ran through conversational Spanish I knew I could get away with but, by the looks of the man, he didn't want to discuss with me how many pets he had or if he often travelled to the City. I'd never wanted Gary to start his shitty quiz more in my life.

"Drink with me Senor," the man suddenly said.

Surprised, but grateful for the breaking of the uncomfortable silence, I forced a smile and raised the glass of San Miguel that Gary had placed in front of me on the sticky bar. I nodded to the man, glass aloft. *Cheers*.

"No, a PROPER drink Senor," and he waved his glass of clear liquid towards Gary who was clearly irritated by the fact that he had been disturbed from organising his picture round.

I watched Gary dump his pile of papers on the bar and turn towards the optics, grabbing for a dusty bottle of Tequila. The man downed his glass and signalled for another. Two shots of glasses were set down in front of us, and I paused to gather myself.

I'm all for some of the hard stuff with some salt and lemon when I'm too drunk to know any better but the last time I'd drunk Tequila straight at 7:30 in the evening I'd ended up crying uncontrollably about the destruction of the rain forests and pissing in my mate's shoe.

"Down the hatch!" I yelped, in as uncool a manner as was humanly possible. I shook my head at myself.

I tried to *not* grab my pint too desperately to wash the tequila away with, and therefore maintain some modicum of masculinity, but my scrunched-up expression and tear rolling down my right cheek almost certainly gave me away. It was then that I saw the collection of shot glasses next to the man. Six or seven at least. This made me feel even more disappointed in my own drinking prowess. I shook my head at myself again.

Julie tried to give me an answer sheet and biro for the quiz, but I waved her away knowing full well that nobody born after the Boer War had a cat in hell's chance of answering any of the questions.

By the time I'd swigged enough of my beer to lose the vomit-inducing taste of the tequila, I was enveloped in the familiar and comforting feeling of 'the buzz'. I felt the day

21

draining away and being replaced by something akin to contentment.

And then, as if sensing the change in my demeanour, "Tequila truly is a gift from God my friend," he said, sliding his tiny glass across to join its many companions.

"I don't trust people who don't drink tequila," he continued. "What are they trying to hide? Tequila self is real self!" I sincerely hoped this wasn't true.

I'd assumed the huge gold watch on the man's wrist had been bought from one of the guys on the beach for 5 Euros but now I noticed the expensive Italian shoes and gold bracelet big enough to anchor a ship and wasn't so sure.

He also had a haircut and beard trim that looked like it would take a team of six barbers a week to complete as well as a designer shirt by someone whose name I couldn't pronounce but had seen in one of Nikki's magazines at some point. I suddenly felt less like I needed to reciprocate in the buying of a round. I caught the back end of a question about Dame Vera Lynn and was comfortable in my decision to not participate in the quiz.

I noticed the man was rhythmically drumming his fingers on the beer mat in front of him and appeared to be considering something. Perhaps he was trying to recall the name of Dame Vera's second-biggest wartime hit but I thought it doubtful.

"Nice watch," I said, as Julie and two more glasses appeared in front of us. I caught myself stealing a glance at her legs as she walked away. It had been a while.

Another uncomfortable silence.

As I wrestled with the decision to repeat myself or turn away and start watching Everton V Bournemouth on a screen behind me, he spoke again. This time more subdued. More considered.

"Would you like to hear a story senor?"

He turned to me for the first time and looked me square in the eyes. Sat so close to each other it was intense and unsettling. If he'd been a woman, I'd have assumed we were on our way to an evening we would both regret tomorrow. Mostly her thought to be honest.

"Why not?" I said jovially, trying to break the tension. "I love a good story."

The man leaned in conspiratorially and lowered his voice further. I found myself glancing up and down the bar, joining in his obvious desire for our conversation to remain private.

"What if I told you three things you won't believe my friend? What if I told you we had met before?"

I sat and waited for the punch line.

"What if I also told you I know everything your heart desires because you yourself have told me and what if I told you I am 46 years old but have been this age since the summer of 1984?"

I continued to wait for the punch line.

And waited.

And waited.

The man didn't flinch but held his stare as if looking for some sort of recognition from me. I was 100% certain we had never met and increasingly certain he was one more night of tequila drinking away from being sat with Crazy Brian.

The heavy silence of the moment was eventually broken by Edith in the corner trying to hide a fart during the music round.

I won't pretend I wasn't slightly unnerved by the lack of irony in the way he delivered his nonsense, and that he didn't look like someone who would ordinarily shout at traffic or wear their Pyjamas to Lidl's, just made it worse. Was there a familiarity? Something in his face tugging at a memory? I didn't think so.

I was famously (annoyingly) good with faces. I would enhance (ruin any enjoyment of) any movie night with Nikki by pointing out all the other things the extras had been in previously.

"Nikki, hey Nikki. That guy, there. The third swordsman from the right. No, the one next to him. Yeah him. He was the dude on the park bench in the Kit Kat advert. Yeah definitely. Pause the film, I'll show you...."

"You don't believe me of course; you'd be insane if you did."

"*You'd know*," I thought.

"But you will, you will my friend." Another shot was gone in a second, and he played an index finger around the top of the empty glass.

"I won't insult your intelligence by telling you your name is Mike Barnes. There are a hundred ways I could know that."

There was. Still weird though.

"But I do know that you only married Nikki because you'd run out of things to talk about and that the real reason

24

you never pushed to have kids with her was that you didn't trust her."

My head spun and I grabbed at the bar to steady myself. I had no idea what the correct response to that was or even what to think. This failed to deter the man.

"I know your Father wanted you to join him in the family business, as did mine, but that you wanted to reach out into the world and achieve great things. As did I. I know that not a day goes by that you don't think about your Mother, even after all these years."

The sheer number of thoughts and feelings rushing in, and just as quickly out again, made it impossible to organise them or focus on one long enough to rationalise it. What he was saying was true. Sure, my close friends would know all of this about me, but I'd never met this guy before in my life.

I'd wanted to be a Pro Golfer rather than join my Dads carpet cleaning business and this was the cause of many a tense moment around the dinner table. Especially as I was shit at golf.

Had I met the guy? Still, something nagged at me amongst the confusion and bewilderment.

"You have started to accept that you will never reach your potential and that scares you more than anything else in the world my friend."

I sat in stunned silence. Everything he'd said was correct.

I searched for an explanation. Nikki would know most of this about me I suppose; had she sent this guy here to mess with me? Why would she? I'd had conversations with my dad before he died last year that got into most of this stuff.

Some even sat in this bar on his last visit before cancer really got hold. Was this guy his ghost or here to pass me a message? Nothing seemed too bizarre as I remained dazed and motionless on the bar stool.

The logical part of my brain stepped in to provide answers. There were people who could perform these tricks by reading an expression or a 'tell'. Who was that guy off the tele? Darren Brown?

Something like that. People made a career out of it. What had he really told me? Really good guesses. That was all. If you said vaguely these same things to enough people, eventually you will be right. Simple maths. Nailed it.

"OK, OK," I said confidently with a wry grin.

"Who DOESN'T want to 'reach their full potential'? And people get married for all sorts of reasons." I allowed myself a less than convincing chuckle and drained what remained of my San Miguel.

"Very impressive 'my friend'." I continued, "But tell me something that wouldn't be true for millions of people sitting in bars like this around the world right now."

As I sat smugly, the man nodded a reluctant acceptance and drummed his fingers once more. An unnerving smile started to stretch across his face.

"The scar behind your left ear."

I subconsciously reached up and touched the ridged and pitted skin. I suddenly felt like I wanted to throw up.

"You tell everyone you got it in a fight with a bully when you were 12."

I already knew he knew.

"But you got it falling off your Mother's high heeled shoes one afternoon when she was at work and hit your head on a coffee table."

Nobody knew that. I'd even told my mum the bully story and seemed to receive some sort of misplaced respect from my parents when I refused to 'grass' the non-existent boy up and chucked in a 'You should see the other guy'.

A headache started to form. I rubbed my temples, eyes squeezed shut, vaguely aware of wanting the man to have been a figment of my imagination, or perhaps sunstroke when I opened them again.

But when I cautiously peeked through a squinted right eye, there he was. As real as the scar on my head.

Chapter 3

I didn't know the guy. 100%. And I had certainly never told him about how when bored one day during the school holidays, I had put on my mum's tallest high heels and walked around my lounge pretending to smoke with a rolled-up 'Breakaway' wrapper. The result of this was a sprained ankle, mild concussion and some street cred I didn't deserve.

Gary was mid-way through a quiz round for which all of the answers were the names of gangster movies. Not that I'd heard any of the questions.

My logical brain, the part that didn't believe in the supernatural, or Gods, or the Bermuda triangle or that Aliens built Stone Henge, or that Elvis was alive and well and living in a council house in Swindon, finally just rolled over and waved the white flag. I simply couldn't explain what the, clearly wealthy, slightly sad looking Spanish guy, was telling me.

"Who are you?" I finally said, having decided that of the questions queuing up in my mind, this was the one I'd start with.

"What's more important to you, my friend, is 'When am I?'"

That I hadn't received a straightforward answer was far from a shock at this stage of proceedings.

"Many years ago, this bar was a Butcher's," he began, turning away from the bar and towards the tables and chairs behind him for the first time. He paused an almost imperceptible fraction of time as if distracted by a memory. He continued in his velvety Spanish accent:

"It was my Father's. I would help out, of course, we all did. My Mother, my Sisters and Brothers, even my Uncles would leave the fields on market day to assist my Father. I feel he always knew I wouldn't join him in the family business when the time came but, where he was certainly disappointed, I felt he always understood, felt he wished he'd maybe had the courage to follow his dreams when he was younger.

"Of course, it was tough back then. I came along as Franco's grip on power was getting tighter and tighter and there wasn't much opportunity for anyone let alone a poor butcher's son, just another in a long line of poor butcher's sons. The problem is, although I tried to spread my wings, tried to expand my horizons, I always found myself back here. A failed marriage, failed businesses, lack of money, always had me crawling back here with my tail between my legs.

"I started to feel 'unworthy', like I didn't deserve any more than I had and would certainly never have any more. I would sabotage jobs, good jobs, relationships, GOOD relationships with good women! I was completely lost. Until one day I was sat outside the shop, sat down in the dirt, right outside where you can see the road is now? I was lighting a

29

*cigarette when a stranger appeared behind me and asked if I
had a light for him also.*

"I had not seen the man before and It was rare to see
someone here that you did not know. Most people were
cousins or related by marriage and you would know the
names of the traders who would pass through.

"He looked tired and well-travelled, his clothes not of a
style I had seen before. He was a young man, hard to age
but I would say in his mid to late twenties.

"I lit my cigarette and passed him the match as he sat
down next to me, dropping a large leather bag onto the dirt
as he did so. I hadn't spoken to the man yet but as he took
long satisfied drags on his cigarette, he began to tell me a
story. Much as I, with you, now.

"I soon forgot the Sun that was beating down on my
shoulders and the mutton, half prepared on the slab at the
back of the shop as the man spoke.

"He knew more about me than I did. Things I hadn't
even admitted to myself or long and very deliberately
forgotten. But he did this for one reason and one reason
only. To show me that when he spoke, he spoke the truth.
Why this was important became apparent when he got to the
real reason that he had sat next to me on that day, in that
place.

"He asked me if I knew how long my Fathers shop had
been there? I explained that it had been in my family for
many generations perhaps five or even six? He asked if I had
known what was on the site before my family had built their
shop here, over a hundred years ago? I did not. He told me
that it had been a Church and for many years, the very*

centre of the community here. He told me however that one day, a holy man had ridden into town.

"He settled into local life and became a friend and confidant of the Pastor here. As time passed, he would even take certain prayers and give sermons for the Pastor. As the story goes, these sermons became more and more passionate and uplifting, inspiring but also terrifying as he burned the words of God's wraths into the congregation.

"When the old Pastor died suddenly (and suspiciously), there was never any doubt that this man would step into his shoes. Rumour has it though that there had been secret 'prayer meetings' with a small number of the locals at this man's house but that some of the interpretations and teachings were controversial shall we say? As time passed, the new Pastor spoke of these teachings and of rituals, which many did not recognise from the scripture that they knew. However, such was his enigmatic charm and energy, people would travel for miles to hear him and the entire congregation would become hypnotised by his words when he would speak.

"When he and others spoke in tongues at Church, it seemed no more than further evidence of his power and affirmation of his being a vessel of God. When he later told people that God had spoken to him directly, people believed him. When he told people that God had demanded sacrifice from them, people believed him.

"When he told the people that God demanded human sacrifice, they believed this also."

"Woah, hold on there just a second," I interrupted. "Let's ignore the fact that you claim to be about eighty years old despite looking younger than me and can, apparently, read my mind and drink enough tequila to put a rugby team down for a week, are you going to tell me that people were sacrificed; actual people? Here?"

The man pushed his hands through his worryingly perfect black hair before continuing.

"I am telling you what the man told me my friend, but no. Apparently, the Pastor had been paying particular attention to a local woman for some time who had a daughter of around twelve or thirteen years. He explained to the woman that God had told him that it was her daughter who was to be the 'gift to God'.

"On the night that the sacrifice was to take place, here, on this spot, in front of the entire village, the girl's father, a well-known local drunk, had apparently run out of rum and reached something akin to sober. He apparently discovered the plan for his daughter and confronted the Pastor. A fight broke out and the girl's father killed the Pastor by stabbing his own crucifix through his heart.

"The incident seemed to bring the locals to their senses and the church was burned to the ground that very same evening, with the Pastors body buried beneath the rubble. The story does continue that when the ruins were cleared sometime later, no body was found."

"Right on this spot?" I said.

"Right on this spot," the man replied.

"Do you believe the story?" I asked, wondering if I believed it or not myself.

"I believe I do my friend. It is not the strangest story I have encountered in my time and perhaps explains certain things from my own story."

There was so little assisting me in keeping even a tentative grip on my usual reality that I felt myself transition into a sense of calm resignation.

"So who was he, the man that told you the story? Why did he tell it to you? More importantly, why are *you* telling *me*?"

The man shuffled on his seat and almost instinctively reached for the glass in front of him. When he found it void of tequila, I saw him make the conscious decision to continue without further lubrication.

"I told him that I was surprised that I had never heard that story before, that I was 46 years old and at one time or another had been told many, many tales by grandparents, aunts and uncles of the history of our town, some true, some clearly not so, many exaggerated but no less intriguing. But never that one. He explained that it was not a period in the town's history its people are proud of.

"Almost killing an innocent young girl? No. It became an unwritten law that the events of that time were never to be spoken of again. The rubble was cleared and buildings quickly constructed on the site, the shame buried below the foundations.

"He asked me more and more questions about my own life and yet I still remember feeling as if he was toying with me, like a cat with a ball of string, like he already knew the answers? I remember that at one point he reached into his bag, pulled out a bottle and poured us both a drink into small glasses that I hadn't noticed on the ground in front of us.

"Sitting there in the middle of my working day drinking tequila with this complete stranger, somehow felt like the most natural thing in the world. He drank and talked, drank and talked. I drank and talked, drank and talked. I emptied my entire sorry life story out on that road.

"I do remember at one point becoming vaguely aware of time pushing on and the mutton that needed butchering being unlikely to butcher itself. He seemed to sense this, although it had not been anything he could have seen, nothing physical, it was just a thought that blew through my mind. He stood and lit another cigarette but after two long drags, threw it into the dirt, rubbed it firmly with his boot and said seven words that would change my life forever:

"I want to make you an offer."

Chapter 4

I recall looking up at him, silhouetted against the sun, faceless. Just a figure in a hat. A figure I hadn't known even ten minutes before. Or an hour before? Two hours? I realised I had no concept of how long I'd been sitting there with the man.

"I can help you," he said. "This is a very special place and you are a very special person. I can't offer this to just anyone." He glanced up and down the street before continuing.

"It is fortunate for me that you have never, how would I put it... never reached your full potential? Well, that is what I am offering you now my friend. The incredible, fantastical, mind-blowingly limitless realisations of that potential."

He stepped back, arms spread wide, a black silhouetted angel against the Alpujarras mountains of my ancestors far in the distance. And I believed him. In that instant, I had complete faith that he could do for me what he said he could. It felt as if my life had led up to that very moment.

That his sitting next to me was in no way a chance. That it had been ordained. That powers I could never even hope to understand had put me on that street, in that dirt, that day, for him to find me. A lamb was found by its shepherd.

"I held my hands out to the man, palms open and empty and just said 'please'."

He explained that I could have everything I had ever dreamed of. Everything my heart desired. That this would come at no cost to me at all but that there were rules. Rules and 'Laws' as he called them.

He advised me not to question the 'offer' or the 'Laws' as it would serve no purpose and be of no help to me. I sat in that dirt and listened to every word he spoke in utter silence.

He said that I would be gifted, and that was the word he used, 'gifted', limitless financial resources. He said I was free to use these resources however I saw fit within the 'Laws'. Houses, cars, planes, jewellery, women, whatever I wanted would be mine.

I could lead a life most men could only dream of. That money would bring me power, influence, friends in high places and all without having to do one more day's work as long as I lived. This money would be available to me whenever and however I wanted it.

"Nice watch," the stranger said, nodding down at my left arm. My watch had been bought at a gas station outside Nerja about five years before and was certainly not of any note. However, as I instinctively looked down at my wrist, there in place of the watch that had cost the same amount as a packet of cigarettes, was not the watch that was sitting on my wrist now.

A solid gold timepiece of a beauty I had never seen before. Its very weight took me by surprise as I raised my hand from my lap. I looked up at the man. The silhouette shrugged back "It's yours. Just to show you that I am all I say I am."

I looked around the bar, suddenly aware that I was becoming part of something secretive, something I was privileged to be hearing, had been CHOSEN to hear. The regulars had clearly become bored of trying to stare the man out of Churchill's and my speaking to him had obviously bought him some time, at least until the end of the quiz. This looked like ending no time soon due to the number of ambiguities being picked up by the couple that won every week.

Gary was looking flustered and frantically trying to clarify some facts on his iPhone with its claret and blue phone case and 'I'm forever blowing bubbles' ring tone. 'Catherine of ARAGON was the first one, it was the other one that survived him!' was bellowed across the length of the establishment by a man whom I had previously been convinced was asleep. People nodded to their partners and chatted to their competitors at the next table while occasionally glaring at Gary.

Gary was doing his best to ignore them due to his level of concentration and typing speed on his phone being equal to that of an elderly sloth trying to solder a circuit board for the Space Shuttle.

I found myself again looking down at the Spanish man's watch. It was exactly as he'd described. A golden, glittering object that seemed to absorb every light source in the room and throw it back out in an array of patterns. I could now *see* the weight, and it was all I could do to not rip it from the man's wrist.

I felt mesmerised by it. I could see every stone encrusted in its precious metal strap, I couldn't pull my eyes away from the hand sweeping around the face and could now see the brand etched across the centre that I somehow hadn't noticed before?

'EL DIABLO'

"And he was…" The Spanish man said although it wasn't clear if he was speaking to me or himself "…he was everything he'd said he was."

A sullen, reflective expression fleetingly swept across his face but it was gone again just as quickly. He idly began rubbing the strap of his watch with his thumb and continued his tale:

He could have told me to do anything at this point, and I would have done it. He became animated, pacing up and down in front of me and telling me of all the things I would see, I would experience, I would OWN. I felt all of my failures and disappointments disappearing with every word he spoke. The man told me who I would become, was *becoming,* even as I sat there in that dirt.

"I must tell you of the… of the conditions, the 'Laws'." The man stopped pacing as he said this and sat so close to me, I could feel him pressed against me. I saw his eyes for the first time properly but as he spoke, they seemed to change from green to blue, to hazel, to deep brown, and I put it down to the changing of the light at the time.

Of all the things that happened that day and since it is his eyes that I remember most clearly, if I close mine now, I can see them like they are in front of me every bit as much as yours are.

Most importantly, he explained, I wasn't to tell anyone where my wealth had come from. I was to give any story I wished but not the truth. Trust funds, lottery wins, fortunate investments, didn't matter.

"Fine," I said, shrugging my shoulders.

I wasn't allowed to give 'life-changing' amounts of money to anyone, whether this is in cash or gifts. This seemed a bit vague to me, but he said I would always 'feel' if I was breaking one of these laws or not. Other than that, he explained, I could do what I wanted.

A million thoughts and feelings were crashing on and through me but every time one of disbelief would clip the wings of the fantasies flying all around, I would see the watch again, and I would believe. I wanted to believe.

I was comfortable with the laws of which he'd spoken, and they seemed little price to pay for such reward. I began to stand but he placed his hand on my leg and pushed me down again as easily as a man could control a small child. Again, I was looking into those chameleon eyes, the blue, the green, the brown, changing, changing, changing. "My friend," he continued.

"You are a man of the world, I see that in you. You know that there is always a... a *price* for the things we want in life?"

I can't remember if I answered him or not, but he continued, nonetheless.

"You will enjoy this great wealth and every object and wonder that your heart desires, but you will do this whilst also remaining exactly as you are now. You will not advance in years."

"I took this in for a second or two."

"I won't age?" I said; this does not seem like a drawback particularly.

"That is correct my friend. You will remain a man of your current age as long as you are enjoying this 'gift'.

"But you will not remain 'You', not the man who sits beside me now."

Of course, I didn't understand. What it turned out he meant was that I would be a completely new person. Different face, different body. Different name. But he wasn't finished.

"And on each anniversary of your transformation, you will change again. Every year regardless of your location or situation."

The more ludicrous these rules became the more I found myself doubting the likelihood of any of it being real. Still, the watch glinted up at me, however.

"But people will notice the changes, surely? People will ask questions?"

"No," he replied enthusiastically. "Because you will also be in a different place. The person you were for the previous 12 months will simply cease to exist and you will find yourself somewhere new. Somewhere new and *exciting*. Think of the possibilities!"

"I was finding it hard to think of anything. My head was swimming with 'laws' and rules and trying in vain to keep some sort of grounding in my own reality. Still, if this wasn't some elaborate joke, the conditions, despite sounding confusing and possibly far from ideal, were more than compensated for by the riches he was promising. And what did I have to lose?"

Back in the bar, the bickering over some of the answers in the Sports round was evolving into something akin to the Cuban missile crisis. Alliances were forming and folding and both Gary's integrity and Father's identity were being brought into question. We should have been deep into the evening's Karaoke by now, much to the annoyance of one or two regulars for whom this was the highlight of their week.

Confusingly, the Spanish man seemed to have stopped telling his story despite me clearly waiting with bated breath for the next instalment.

"…and?" I said, leaning in closer.

He turned to me and held his arms out loosely to his sides, motioning for me to observe his clothes, his shoes, his watch.

"What do *you* think? I said 'YES' of course. I am sitting here in front of you having to lead the lives of many men. I have seen things you would give anything to see. Done things you would not believe. Been loved by Women… Women, you would die for one night with."

I glanced across at Julie once more and wondered how attractive a woman would have to be for that to be the case for me at this point in time.

When I think back to that conversation now, it seems incredible that I didn't just write the guy off as a crackpot, but the Tequila and Beer had done a reasonable job of making it all sound almost plausible.

"Let's say for one moment I believe you, or even that I think you are one cerveza short of a six-pack. Doesn't matter. How did you know those things about me? About Nikki? About my life?"

Another wry grin broke across his face.

"Last year. You travelled to Barcelona with a friend to watch a football match."

He wasn't asking. He was *telling* me.

"You never made it to the game as you got too drunk in a bar near to the stadium on the way. Your friend collapsed and slept under a table and you spent the afternoon sitting telling your life story to a man you met at the bar."

There it was. The nagging feeling I'd had earlier in the evening was back with more intensity and as the man sat with his eyes boring into mine, I realised why. I *had* met him before. But not him. Not THIS him.

I did recall the evening. Or parts of it. I still had the unused tickets for the game in my kitchen draw at home. Now I had a reference point I realised that plenty about the man was familiar. But certainly not the man himself.

It was becoming harder to not accept the absurd truth of the situation.

"I am not a mind reader my friend. You have told me all of the things I told you, before. In Barcelona. Almost a year ago to the day."

Once you accept the unexplainable, the miraculous, and as much as it pains me to say it, the paranormal even, there is an electricity that shoots through you. Like you have been plugged into energy that you couldn't access before. It's as if your mind opens up. Like a flower trying to absorb all the sunlight, it can get.

Nothing appears the same anymore. Like a bulb going on in a dimly lit room. That's how it felt sitting in Churchill's that night. That's how it felt for me.

I believed him. The trouble was my brain couldn't make the connections quickly enough, couldn't prioritise what question to ask first, what was important and what wasn't. I went for the basics.

"What's your name?" I asked.

"My current name? Diego. Diego Los Rios. My *actual* name? It seems to have so little meaning now, but it was

Sergio Martinez. That was the name above the door of my Fathers shop. '*Martinez y Hijos*'. Martinez and Sons."

Diego, as I would call him for the duration that I knew him, took a bundle of notes from his trouser pocket as he rose from his seat, and tossed them onto the bar.

"Let's walk my friend."

I followed him as he took a route from the bar that would take us back towards the seafront. Although it was now late, the town was illuminated with the neon lights of restaurants and tapas bars, gift shops and children's arcades.

I'd walked this very route a hundred times but felt like I was seeing it for the first time. Lights were brighter, Palm tree's loomed larger, and I could *feel* people's laughter and chatter as we passed them.

I noticed Diego would sweep his long hair up and away from his face every few moments, and he saw me watch him do it.

"I've never got used to this hair. I suppose I could have cut it short but it feels like it's part of 'Diego'. Still, not long to go now."

We continued to make our way towards the rhythmic sound of the Mediterranean Sea, calmly rolling up and down the beach that in a matter of weeks would be a mass of sardined holidaymakers.

"By the time I met you in Barcelona I was starting to feel that my time was done. I felt stretched thin somehow. Although my body was, *is,* that of a middle-aged man, my mind grows weary. I am 82 years old. The life that the 'gift' has given me, I no longer have the mental energy to enjoy it."

He stopped both walking and speaking for just a second, and I was aware of the rustling of the giant palm leaves above me.

"Tired. I'm just tired."

Diego set off again, and I followed in step with him.

"There was another 'Law' that the stranger passed onto me, that day sat in the dirt. He said that the 'gift' was mine and mine alone and would always be so until I gave it away and it was willingly accepted by another. Michael, I'd like to give it to you."

This was a pivotal moment in the journey of my life and one that would shape my very existence, my very *being*, forever. We had exited a small side road and emerged at a raised section of the promenade, the perfectly linear horizon stretching incomprehensibly into the distance to both my right and my left.

The enormity of the ocean overwhelmed me, its vastness weighing down on me underneath the infinite, intimidating, blackness of the night sky. Things would never be the same again. I turned to Diego.

"Yeah. Alright then."

Admittedly my response hadn't exactly ranked up there with Dr King's *I Have a Dream* or Armstrong's *One Giant Leap*, but in my defence, I'd consumed a reasonable amount of alcohol, it was late, and ultimately, I probably still didn't really believe a lot of what he was saying.

Diego sat himself down on the wall that separated the beach from the pedestrianised promenade behind it. I followed suit and we both swung our legs over to be facing the Ocean.

"I appreciate this is a lot to take in Michael and your questions must be many, perhaps you even still have doubts about what I have told you? But I do need to know if you will accept my 'offer'."

"Look," I responded. "It's a great story, and, OK, I can't explain some of the stuff you've told me tonight. Do I want you to be telling the truth? Yeah, I suppose I do. Does something at my very core, for some inexplicable reason, believe you? Yes. Yes, it does. But it can't be true, it just can't be. I don't know what to say to you."

I shrugged and turned away. The graffiti on the wall, some cigarette butts on the sand below, some music from a bar further down the promenade, all helped ground me a little.

Unfortunately, as I turned back to Diego, the light from the moon was reflecting back to me off of his watch and made it look like it was ablaze. It felt more than just coincidence, even at the time.

"Theoretically Michael, if everything I was saying was true? If I could pass this 'gift' to you and you would wake up tomorrow the wealthiest man ever to have walked upon this Earth? What would you say?"

I thought about it for as long as it took one roll of the tide to push its way up the beach towards me.

"I'd say yes. Why wouldn't I? My life is a 'Groundhog Day' of swimming pools and drinking too much. I have no girlfriend, no real friends here, I'm sure what little family I have back home haven't even realised I don't live in England anymore. Theoretically… I'd say yes."

"Would you shake my hand on that my friend?" Diego said with an urgency he struggled to disguise as he shoved a tanned and manicured hand in front of me. This of course made me instinctively reluctant but hey, it was theoretical right? And this whole thing was just crazy, wasn't it? Maybe even a stupid bet Diego had with a friend to make some idiot foreigner shake hands on this nonsense offer? That was probably it.

"Yeah, sure," I said. A minuscule amount of time before my palm met him however, I noticed the watch again. It's easy for your memory to play tricks on you, especially in such bizarre circumstances, but it was glowing. Pulsating even.

As the light from the moon hit it, I would swear it changed from gold to green to blue and a rainbow of other colours. My hesitation at this point was of no consequence as he planted his hand firmly into mine.

The last thing I remember of that evening was a look in Diego's eyes.

You could have said it was sorrow but as strong an argument that it was the very opposite. Relief? Very likely. Guilt?

I certainly grew to hope so.

Chapter 5

Even without opening my eyes, it was obvious I'd forgotten to close the blinds before going to bed the previous evening. This wasn't helping the headache that was threatening to force me up and hunting for Ibuprofen when all I wanted to do was drift off for another couple of hours. At least I hadn't spent any of my own money on the tiny man who had climbed into my head and was playing the bongos on my brain. No, the night had been free of charge courtesy of the friendly but unhinged Spanish guy I'd met in the bar.

The finer details were a tad blurry, but I hadn't drunk so much I couldn't recall the crux of the conversation. I allowed myself a small smile as I tried to pull the covers up over my head to block out the light streaming through the window.

'Not your regular Friday night' I thought to myself.

I decided that I had allowed myself to get sucked into the guy's crazy story due to a mixture of alcohol and boredom. What was the alternative? Gary's quiz? An early return to the apartment getting frustrated with the blocks communal Satellite dish not working again? Nope, no regrets. Very entertaining. Worth the headache and not being able to remember walking home.

At all.

Which did suddenly strike me as strange.

The pain in my head was from mixing drinks, not so much the quantity consumed and so I certainly hadn't blacked out in any way. Either way, for the time being, I had bigger fish to fry. Could I get from bed to window to close the blind without opening my eyes, crawl back again and sleep off the headache? It was a mission I felt I could execute successfully.

I had stumbled around in the dark of my bedroom in various states of inebriation on many occasions so this should be a walk in the park.

I pushed back the duvet, exposing my naked body to the otherwise empty apartment and gingerly placed my feet down on the cold tiles. Eyes firmly shut I patted around for my flip flops which I always kept by my bed. Failing to locate them, I bravely continued my quest.

I was now facing my bed, hunched over and feeling my way along the length of it towards the foot. It seemed to go on forever. Just a trick of the mind caused by not having the reference points sight would ordinarily give.

I reached the end, stood, turned ninety degrees, and headed across the void of the floor, arms outstretched for protection from smashing my face into the window, or a wall if I'd miscalculated direction when I set off.

I started to become concerned that I was heading out of my bedroom door and would potentially find myself toppling over my balcony into the car park two floors below, such as the length of time it was taking me to reach the far wall of my tiny apartment. However, just as I was about to be forced to open an eye a smidge, I felt my fingertips press against the glass. 'Phase one complete' I thought.

Despite my bedroom looking out onto rooftops and air-conditioning units, I still felt marginally self-conscious being stood in my window with the family jewels on full display. Especially with it being unseasonably chilly on this particular morning.

I, therefore, quickened my pace and began to crab across the window to its left edge where the chord for the blind limply hung. I couldn't help but make the obvious comparison.

I took a sidestep and reached out my hand expecting to feel the chord or window frame. Nothing. Just more glass. I started to wonder if last night's Tequila had been an 'Alice in Wonderland-esque' shrinking potion, and I was now a tiny man navigating my way around my now relatively giant room. Still, I was determined to try and maintain a state of semi-slumber and give myself the best chance of falling back to sleep on completion of the mission.

Another sidestep.

And another.

Still no chord, still no window frame.

With a full and exasperated sigh, I surrendered my mission as a failure and resigned myself to squinting through one eye to locate the chord of my dusty Venetian blind. I simultaneously berated the stupid Spanish sky for always being unnecessarily clear and sunny and bright.

Unfortunately, part opening one eye didn't help, as my brain couldn't make sense of what it was seeing. I had to open the second for clarification.

The window I was stood in front of was eight feet high, floor to ceiling, approximately 20 feet wide and instead of some scruffy rooftops and the odd feral cat, my view was from a position that looked to be about 20 floors up and looked directly down onto a recognisably iconic, unmistakable, hustling and bustling City.

The Las Vegas strip.

The faux Eiffel Tower of hotel 'Paris', the Pyramid of the 'Luxor' far off down the boulevard and to my right, Caesars Palace and the water ballet fountains of the Bellagio. A helicopter suddenly appeared from the right side of the window and noisily swept around in front of me at eye level before disappearing again around the back of whatever the hell hotel I appeared to be stood in, naked, staring down at a place I had only ever seen on TV and in Movies.

I squeezed my eyes firmly shut again and became aware that I was on the verge of passing out through hyperventilation. I felt my knees buckle, and I dropped forward, supporting myself on the huge pane of glass. After a moment to gather myself, I genuinely expected to open my eyes and it all have been some illusion caused by too much drink or whatever mine had been spiked with by the crazy Spanish dude.

I was jolted back into the room by the sound of the man-made Volcano at the front of the 'Mirage' hotel, booming into life.

I took a startled step back and could now see a faintly transparent reflection of my naked body in the window.

This did not help to ease my sense of panic.

It wasn't me.

I looked down at the body. It was a shade or two darker than mine and *felt* shorter. I was usually 6'2" in my flip flops but I was definitely closer to the floor as I stood there. There were some upgrades, however. It was more muscular, toned and had a neat swathe of chest hair as opposed to my usual half dozen Nikki had sarcastically given individual names to one Sunday morning in bed.

A thunderbolt of thought hit me, and I slowly leaned forward, peering tentatively downwards. Down past my new chest hair and subtle six-pack…

Definitely an upgrade.

My face. Christ, what if I have all this but the 'catch' is a face like smashed avocado?

I turned to find a mirror and saw the room for the first time. It was the size of a tennis court. Far bigger than my apartment. The bed that had felt big as I crawled my way along it, *was* big. Enormous. Enormous and about fifteen yards away.

Just from where I stood, I could see four TVs the size of cinema screens. There was a dining table large enough to seat 16 people comfortably, a jacuzzi you could fall out of bed and straight into and even a leather-bound, mahogany and felt topped poker table perched on a raised level to my left. Expensive looking Italian art adorned the walls and heavy, oversized furniture from glass tables to Chaise Lounges filled spaces on the marble floor. The Penthouse suite.

I became aware of my state of undress and grabbed a silk dressing gown that was strewn over an ornate, high back chair.

Making my way across the room towards a huge free-standing mirror in the corner, the realisation that the previous evenings theoretical had become today's reality, engulfed me entirely. How did I feel? Disorientated but excited? What surprised me was that there was no sense of loss. What had I left behind? I allowed myself a moment to stop and take it all in. I stood, hands-on hips in the middle of that vast room and just smiled a smug smile to myself.

I was, however, trying to ignore the underlying nervousness of seeing my new face for the first time. Brad Pitt or swamp pit?

My smile became near hysterical laughter as I saw the stubbled and square jawline of the new me. A strong but proportionately sized nose, dark brooding eyes and a mouth I wanted to kiss myself. Somewhere between George Clooney and Joey from 'Friends' was the best comparison I could make.

Result. 'I could do some damage with this' I thought to myself as I eyed the new me up and down.

I had a sudden urge to call someone, to share this amazing thing with another person and spun towards the phone by the boat sized bed.

Two thoughts conspired to spoil my otherwise extremely positive mood. I had nobody to call. Nobody would scream back at me in excitement and ask a million questions that would need answering. I briefly thought about calling Nikki and gloating in some way, but the second thought stopped me from doing so before it had really morphed into a practical idea.

"...and you can't contact anyone from your previous life. It's one of the 'Laws'..."

I managed to shake off the empty feeling that was threatening to attach a cloud to my silver lining and made my way curiously to an annexe I'd spotted that was positioned back towards the window along the same wall as the bed. It was a dressing room.

Row after row of designer suits and expensive-looking shirts. Shelves packed full of jeans and T-shirts. In the middle of this room, with railings set out like a horseshoe, was a set of draws stuffed full with a department store's amount of sunglasses, cufflinks and assorted jewellery laid out neatly within.

And there, in its own section in the very centre of the top draw, was the watch.

Even in the semi-gloom of that dressing room, it shone every bit as brightly as it had in the moonlight on Diego's wrist. I held it in my hand for the first time. 'El Diablo' across the face in calligraphic text, diamonds around its rim and along the length of the otherwise solid gold strap.

I opened the clasp and slid the object onto my arm. Its weight was reassuring, validating, empowering. The cold metal against my wrist was confirmation that what I was experiencing was real. I searched for other 'reality anchors'. I could feel the soft draft of air-conditioned air against my neck. Hear subtle 'hotel' noises behind the walls. Felt the tailored fabric of one of the many suits as I drew it through my fingertips.

"Let's do this," I said to myself out loud, grabbing for a pair of silk boxer shorts so smooth I could barely pick them up.

I swiftly concluded dressing with a short sleeve shirt and trousers combo; smart but with an eye on the fact that it looked to be about a hundred degrees outside. Without admitting it to myself, I think I also wanted people to be able to see the watch that would leave no doubt as to the wealth of its owner.

OK.

Women.

Leave no *Women* with any doubt as to the wealth of its owner.

Having tied the laces on a pair of shoes that looked expensive enough to require their own security, I strode confidently from the dressing room.

Money.

Looking this great was all well and good but they weren't going to let me trade an enigmatic smile and some perfectly coiffured hair for poker chips.

I couldn't see a big pile of cash on a table or Platinum credit card next to the bed. So how did this work then? I rooted through some draws, opened some cupboards, even looked behind some cushions on one of the sofas. Nothing.

Frustrated and confused, I stopped, sighed, and shoved my hands in my pockets. But it wasn't just my hand in the left side pocket. I pulled out a small leather wallet. On opening it, I found two things. A driver's licence in the name of 'Marcus Taylor' and a Gold credit card bearing the same name issued by 'Banco Deabru'. The face on the driver's licence was mine. My new face anyway.

"So I'm a *Marcus* then, am I?" I nodded to myself. "I can be a Marcus."

In the other pocket was a hotel key card. 'The Palazzo' was emblazoned across the front. 'Guess that's where I am then?' I thought as I slid the key card into the wallet alongside the driver's licence.

I made my way across the remaining thirty feet of marbled floor and intermittent Persian rugs and up to two steps towards the imposing double doors of the suite.

With one last check of my perfect teeth and hair, I swung the door open with a purpose I felt befitting the occasion.

"Jesus Christ!" I squealed, as I stumbled backwards, barely preventing myself from crashing down the steps behind me.

"Not exactly," said my pool cleaning employee Juan, who was standing in the doorway of the suite in front of me. Large as life. In Las Vegas. Dressed in full evening wear and tails.

I'd dropped to my backside and was looking up at Juan who had stepped into the suite and was offering his hand to help me up off the floor.

I couldn't do anything but stare at him. The power of speech had deserted me entirely.

In a confused daze, I took his hand and managed to stand. I couldn't take my eyes off of him as my brain struggled to make sense of what I was seeing.

"Wuh? Howww? Whhhho?" was all I could muster.

Juan pushed the door closed behind him, skipped down the steps and straight over to a heavy mahogany cabinet next to the bed. He flicked it open and rubbed his hands together before pulling out a bottle of Scotch from what must have been the Penthouse Suite equivalent of the mini-bar.

Grabbing two tumblers from a tray on top of the cabinet, he swept back over to where I was standing, gave me a mischievous grin and sat himself down on the steps with a thump.

"Come on, Mike! Or should I say *Marcus…*" he said with a conspiratorial wink and a nod "…never known you to turn down a drink!" His hard Spanish accent had gone and had been replaced by something resembling Dick Van Dykes attempt at Cockney.

He patted the floor with his hand as if directing a small child or a dog.

As I sat, he handed me a large glass of twenty-year-old Scotch.

"How ya doin', Boss?" he said through an expanding smile.

I shrugged and shook my head, still trying to make sense of his being there.

"I have no idea, to be honest Juan. What the FUCK are you doing here? And *why* do you sound like that?"

"I'm your butler! Comes with the 'High Roller' suite! Cool, eh?"

"Yeah, I suppose," I said. "I meant more what are *you* doing here? HOW are you here?"

Juan stood up, swilling his scotch around in his glass.

"It's like this. I was never just your dashing young pool cleaner and scourge of many a resort bedroom. We had our eye on you for a while. It was my job to observe and report back and see if you could be 'our guy'."

"Your guy?" I asked, without comprehension of what that meant.

"Exactly. Look, you don't need to know the borrrring detail of all this, just be excited that you have it! I'm here to keep you on the straight and narrow, make sure none of those pesky 'Laws' is broken." He winked at me for the second time since he'd been in the room which was the most disturbing thing about the whole scenario.

"I'll only be there when you need me. The consequences of breaking the 'laws' can be, well, unpleasant to say the least. But you don't need to worry about that! You're a bright guy, you'll be fine!"

The excitement of my situation was waning slightly the more Juan spoke.

I stood and paced. My head felt as if it was full of cotton wool, and I struggled to formulate a single thought. It was all feeling a bit sinister suddenly. 'Unpleasant' consequences he'd said? 'THEY' whoever 'THEY' are, had been watching me for some time. Juan had worked for me for two years. Two years! And the make of the watch hadn't completely passed me by 'El Diablo' The Devil. Had Diego and I met by chance in Barcelona? Who was Juan really? WHAT was Juan really?

Before I could try and answer any of these questions myself, Juan topped my glass up, despite me not having drunk any of the Scotch already in it.

"Get some of that down ya, Boss, you'll feel a whole lot better!"

I looked down at the near-full tumbler.

"I'm not sure it's a good idea, I need to get my head straight for a minute, need to…to work out what's going on…"

"Trust me," Juan said, stepping forward, putting his hand under my glass and pushing it up towards my mouth. His gaze didn't move from mine.

I resisted slightly.

"TRUST ME..." he repeated.

A hit of alcohol suddenly felt far from the worst idea, and I gulped a mouthful down. And a second. And a third.

Juan was stood grinning at me, wide-eyed and fidgety.

"Annnd..." he said, winking at me for the third time.

"Stop winking at me, Juan, it's making me feel uncomfortable and... and..."

I was stopped by an unfamiliar sensation. I'd got through plenty of Scotch in my time, but this was different. A calm positivity that seemed to start at my feet and make its way up my body soon became a feeling of confidence. The confidence became something else.

Arrogance? Power? I looked down at the glass and felt indestructible. That I *deserved* all this wealth and good fortune. That under different circumstances I would have got here myself. That this was the Universe simply correcting itself. "That's right," I said aloud "I *should* have all this."

"Yes, you should, Boss. Yes, you should," Juan said, as he opened the door to the hotel suite and stood aside to let me pass.

The lift doors opened onto the main Casino floor and an onslaught of the senses. Slot machines whirred and flashed and tempted people in with the promise of untold riches, a bar was surrounded by enticing games to play while you drank your complimentary drinks and a multitude of machines beckoned gamblers in like the mythological Sirens luring Sailors to the rocks.

Faces were a mixture of concentration, despair, ecstasy and acceptance. Roulette table after roulette table of croupiers hoovering up client's chips only for them to be immediately replaced by more. People couldn't surrender their hard-earned cash quickly enough. The house always wins.

"*Until now*," I thought, as I stood on the edge of the Casino floor and surveyed my Empire.

"What are you thinking, Boss?" Juan said, craning his neck for a better view of the electronic landscape.

"Blackjack," I said confidently.

We strode across the room towards an area that housed row after row of Blackjack tables. Every table was packed with eager players, every few seconds a cheer would go up from someone hitting a '21'. There was irresistible energy, I could feel my heart quickening and adrenalin starting to course through my body. We passed the lower stakes tables, then the mid-stake tables until we reached an area that was cordoned off and had a smartly dressed guy roughly the size of a family car, who stood controlling entry and exit.

As we approached the walking, talking Ford Focus, I opened my mouth to ask about entry to what was obviously the 'High Stakes' area. However, before I could get a word out, Juan and the Ford exchanged a 'nod' and the heavy red rope was removed from my path.

"Good evening, Mr Taylor, and good luck," the Ford Focus said in a voice so deep it made Barry White sound like Joe Pasquale, and I passed into the area where the clients seemed to be more subdued than on the tables now behind me.

"Oh, thanks," I said, once I remembered he was talking to me.

Juan ushered me over towards a table that had three other people sitting at it, each slightly obscured by the huge pile of chips in front of them. The hands of the dealer moved quicker than I could keep up with and cards were on the table before I was even able to add up their totals. Regardless, I felt like a winner. I had no doubt my considerable experience of Blackjack would bring this place to its knees, especially with the resources at my disposal.

My entire Blackjack career, however, amounted to one night in a Casino in Watford, on my cousins Stag do when I lost fifty quid, fell off my stool blind drunk and got thrown out.

The Scotch was still doing its intended job as I took one of the empty seats at the table.

An attractive and clearly wealthy lady, perhaps in her mid-50s, smiled at me politely as the dealer whisked away some of her chips. The jewellery dripping from her wrist clinked as she raised her champagne glass from the table and took an elegant sip.

Between myself and the woman, was a large guy in a suit but wearing ornate cowboy boots and a Stetson to complete the ensemble. He was more animated than the other two and looked on the brink of a coronary, as another pile of his chips disappeared onto the dealer's side of the table. He did manage a 'Hey' at me in a heavy Texan accent whilst nervously fiddling with his remaining funds.

The third person barely looked old enough to be in a Casino and was sat in a hoody with the drawstrings pulled and dark sunglasses covering what little of his face was visible. He didn't flinch as I sat next to him and certainly didn't acknowledge my arrival. He could have been asleep if not for the constant flicking out of high-value chips onto the felt.

All movement at the table then stopped. I sat and waited before becoming aware that the Texan and the older woman were glancing at me between sips of their drinks.

"Sir?" the dealer said.

I looked up at him innocently for a second.

"Yeah, sorry, course!" I replied, disappointed by how quickly I had lost any potential credibility amongst my fellow gamblers.

Before I could become any more flustered, Juan tapped me on the shoulder.

"There you go Mr Taylor," He said, handing me a wedge of hundred-dollar bills that would have paid most people's mortgages off.

I looked up at Juan, and he flashed me the now-familiar grin. I took the brick of notes and passed it to the dealer. They were gone below the table in the blink of an eye and replaced with a stack of Casino chips. I could see that they were in denominations from $500 to $5000.

The game continued again with the dealer's hands a blur across the green felt, and I often struggled to work out if I'd won or lost before the dealer had taken, or added to, the chips I was gambling.

Occasionally, the Texan would clap me on the back, which I took as a good sign, and the bejewelled woman would smile and nod in my direction. Twenty minutes in, and I was getting the hang of it. Increasing my bets when on a good run and playing more cautiously when I wasn't. My stack of chips seemed to have remained roughly where I'd started.

Fresh glasses of champagne would appear in my drinks holder, often before the last was even finished. After an hour or so, hoody's stack had doubled in size, and he casually stood, flicked a $1000 chip at the dealer as 'tip' and strolled away to what looked like a private Poker room in another cordoned off area of the Casino. Texan however had twice disappeared, presumably to plunder a cash machine or speak to whoever made decisions on lines of credit, and I genuinely hoped he could afford to absorb the losses he was taking.

The lady among us seemed to have a reduced pile of chips but nothing too alarming. She was relaxed and self-assured, taking the losses as graciously as the wins. After Texans third skyscraper of chips had quickly become a bungalow, he pushed all he had left into the betting area in front of him.

The dealer hesitated just a second longer than usual and dealt the cards. Texan had a Jack and an eight. Eighteen. Not the worst by any stretch. I busted when I should have 'stuck' and our female friend was sitting out the hand, lighting a cigarette and typing something on her phone.

The dealer turned over a seven and a five. Texan stood up. He clearly felt his night rested on the turn of the next card.

King of Hearts.

The dealer had busted.

Texan whooped, and I was forced to high five him for the thirtieth time that evening.

"That's what I'm talking about!" He bellowed in his Confederate drawl, before scooping up his winnings and tossing a 'tip' to the dealer.

"Thank you, ladies and gentlemen, and I bid you good night," he said, touching the brim of his hat and striding away.

He had probably lost something close to a hundred thousand dollars over the course of the evening. I guess that's the beauty of gambling and its best buddy, denial.

A few more hands and another flute of champagne came and went.

"Australian?" the woman and only other player now at the table suddenly said, stubbing out her cigarette in an expensive-looking ashtray.

I had been trying to count my chips but the alcohol had taken its toll on my mastery of arithmetic. Squinting didn't seem to help.

"Err, no, English actually. American?" I asked in reply.

"Canadian," she replied with an engaging smile.

I noticed for the first time what a classically beautiful woman she was. She must have had them falling at her feet in her absolute prime and probably still got plenty of attention even now.

Between hands, we began chatting about everything from gambling to travel, to loves lost and plans for the future. Obviously, a significant amount of what I was saying was absolute bollocks, completely invented to fit my new persona. Occasionally, Juan would step in to help out if I sounded like I was going to trip up and give something away. This was obviously one of his many functions and one he performed with aplomb, Raquel, as it transpired was her name, never suspected a thing.

"So how is someone as good looking and successful as yourself, owner of the world's second-largest shoe-lace Empire, single and drinking on his own?"

I found myself blushing with the 'good looking' comment but turned briefly and glared at Juan. He had interjected earlier in the evening when Raquel had asked 'what is it you do?'.

Shoelaces apparently.

"I guess I'm just lucky," I said jovially.

She laughed and held my gaze for just a little bit too long.

I felt the beginning of stirrings I barely recognised.

The dealer flicked the cards out and the conversation continued, now tickling at the edges of flirtatious.

A woman like that wouldn't even notice me under normal circumstances, let alone be giving me bedroom eyes, and I started to appreciate more of the advantages Marcus Taylor was going to have over Michael Barnes.

With my newfound confidence and pre-existing 'boy next door' charm that had been all I'd had in my armoury for chatting up Women until I'd woken up this morning, the night started to gain an air of inevitability. I would tell a witty, mostly invented, anecdote, and she would giggle and tell me how funny I am, as Americans and Canadians tend to do. Time wore on and the pattern repeated itself as often as the champagne was replaced and consumed.

At one point, Raquel twisted towards me in her seat and crossed her legs one over the other while reaching in her bag for a decorative cigarette case. This whole process took very slightly too long and was clearly for my benefit. I wasn't sure how much longer I could keep up the game. Fortunately, I needn't have worried.

"My race is nearly run I'm afraid Mr Shoelace King."

I glared at Juan again who had already turned away, pretending he hadn't heard.

"How about we call it a day but, if I lose one last hand, we'll say goodnight and go our merry way but if I win, you can show me the view of the strip from your room. I hear it's something to behold from the Penthouse suite?"

We looked at each other for a moment while the dealer shuffled the cards and didn't bother trying to hide a smile. Just another night at the Vegas tables.

Juan pretended to see something he needed to attend to and wandered away from the table.

"Sounds good to me," I said, holding her gaze and hoping I looked suitably nonchalant, despite shifting in my seat and trying to ignore the beginnings of a stiffy.

Raquel pulled a '16' and I held my breath. The dealer showed 10 clubs. I could tell he was rooting for me and took slightly longer to turn his second card.

Seven of diamonds.

Raquel had lost.

No Penthouse shenanigans.

I just froze in my seat.

"Best of three?" she said with a grin.

Chapter 6

When I woke up, it took me a few moments to get my bearings. Then everything flooded back in like a tsunami of information, and I had to work hard to arrange it in order I could make sense of.

I allowed myself a smug nod of acknowledgement as I eventually recalled the two and a half hours before I'd collapsed exhausted on the giant bed. 'There's no substitute for experience' I said to the room, Raquel having showered and left some hours before. I had been well and truly used by her for her entertainment and pleasure.

Long may that continue.

I walked over to the window and looked down on what was now Las Vegas by night. This is what it was built for. Neon lights, giant illuminated wheels, electronic billboards advertising everything from Celine Dion concerts to adult-only shows, everywhere you looked something was trying to persuade you to part with whatever cash you might have left.

I decided to go for a stroll and see it in all its glory. I'd thoroughly enjoyed my first few hours as a squillionaire but the world had become my giant playground and I'd so far spent all of my time in the same hotel. Juan was nowhere to be seen but I showered, dressed, grabbed the wallet which was now stuffed with notes as well as the credit card and headed into the mayhem.

I wandered from hotel to hotel for hours. Every single one was a scene from a movie I'd watched. My pockets were bulging with the cards of call girls, what with me being too British and too polite to decline them when thrust into my hand on the street.

With nowhere in particular to be, I stood for an hour watching the various choreographed performances of the Bellagio fountains. It was hard not to feel a sense of wonder and awe as they boomed their watery performers twenty stories high before they rained back to the man-made lake below.

I looked at my watch, saw the fountains dancing in its face and a million lights reflected back at me.

10:37 p.m.

This time yesterday I had been sitting in Churchill's wondering what institution Diego had absconded from. To say it felt a lifetime ago would in no way be an overstatement.

I started to formulate something like a plan. I decided to make a list of things I wanted to do, *could do,* with the resources at my disposal.

I turned away from the fountains and beyond the trees that lined this section of the boulevard, the Eiffel Tower stood, illuminated and dominating the skyline. I'd seen an advert on one of the billboards for the bar at the top of the tower and decided it would be a good place to start my journey proper. I'd never been to Paris.

I made my way across the eight lanes of traffic and up to the viewing deck of the tower on the 11th floor. As I approached the entrance to the restaurant a friendly looking, overtly camp chap in stereotypically French dress of tight trousers and stripy top, practically bounced in front of me and blocked my way in.

"Sorry, sir, we are fully booked, do you have a reservation?"

I peered over the Concierge's shoulder and could see that although it was indeed busy and most of the tables were occupied, there were one or two sat vacant, including a booth at the very back with a window facing down the Strip.

"How about that one?" I asked, pointing to the empty booth.

"I am afraid that one is reserved for our *VIP* guests, sir," the man replied with a fake, constipated smile and condescending tone. If he had patted me on the head, I would have felt less patronised.

Perhaps if he had been less of a bellend, I might have walked away, but something about his manner had riled me up. I paused only momentarily.

I pulled out my wallet and the thick wedge of hundred-dollar bills from within it. I pulled down the oversized menu he was holding in both hands until it was horizontal. The Concierge looked slightly confused and concerned but before he could pull it away again, I began dealing the bills onto the menu like playing cards. One hundred, two hundred, three hundred…

"I *totally* understand…" I said, equally as patronisingly.

"…but I'm *really* hungry."

…four hundred, five hundred, six hundred…

"Perhaps I could speak to your manager or someone else that can help me…?"

…seven hundred, eight hundred, nine hundred dollars.

As quickly as the professional dealers at the Blackjack table had swept up the losing chips, the Concierge swiped the notes away and stuffed them in a, now bulging back pocket, of the already-stretched trousers. With a swift, nervous check of whom may have seen our little transaction, he clasped the menu to his chest and turned on his heels.

"Right this way, sir," he said with bright eyes and a vastly more genuine smile. "I think we may have just had a cancellation."

I sat in the booth staring down the Strip towards the 'Stratosphere', the tallest building in Vegas. Eight hundred feet above the ground, its restaurant spun imperceptibly as I tapped a pen on a blank piece of paper borrowed from the Concierge. What did I want to do with all this money? Not being able to change anyone's life with it took away the option of becoming some sort of Saintly benefactor to the world's needy that, as nice as that would have been, was a bit of a relief in terms of decision making.

My previous charity work had amounted to sponsoring a work colleague's five-year-old daughter to see how many times she could run around her garden in ten minutes. Fortunately for me, she threw up her lunch on the eighth time around and had to call it a day.

My wishes were permitted to be completely selfish. Guilt-free.

However, ten minutes later my list read as follows:

Buy fuck off house
Buy a really cool car
Buy a wicked guitar

Learn to play the guitar

Buy a giraffe

I cursed my lack of imagination.

I was grateful when a disturbance at the entrance to the restaurant distracted me. Two men were arguing with the manager and the Concierge and gesturing in my general direction. One of them looked awful like Elton John, whom I had seen was resident at one of the Hotels, but it was hard to be sure from the distance I was from them. Apparently, someone had taken their table.

"Need a hand?" Juan said chirpily, sliding himself into the booth and whipping the list away from me.

"Where did you come from?" I asked, wondering how I hadn't seen him until he was sitting opposite me.

"Now THAT'S the million-dollar question, isn't it, Marcus?" Juan chuckled to himself while shaking his head disappointingly at my list.

I tore it away from him.

"I've only just started," I lied, turning my face down on the table.

"You've been here half an hour! And what do you want a Giraffe for?"

"It's my list, now piss off unless you are going to help."

"Ah, I wish I could, your year will be done by the time you come up with anything exciting. Right, what are we having then?" he said, hunched over the menu, brow furrowed.

"I could eat a horse…or a Giraffe!" he rocked back in his seat and laughed out loud at my expense again. Knob head.

We ordered enough food to feed a large hungry family and Juan drank a swimming pools volume of Mojitos while I pondered my list. I also resisted the temptation to ask Juan the deeper questions, the giant Elephant in the room, about how any of this was possible. I knew I wouldn't get a straight answer, and I figured there would be plenty of time for that.

Juan gurgled the last, icy, dregs of a drink down as I stared despairingly at the Strip below for inspiration. My list had grown to include an aeroplane, possibly with my face on, and a Football Club. But that was as far as I'd got.

I just couldn't concentrate long enough to try and imagine any of this becoming a reality. Something scratched and poked away at the edge of my consciousness and no matter how hard I tried to ignore it, it refused to let me fully engage in the task at hand.

"Go on then."

I looked up at Juan.

"Go on then," he said again.

"*Go on* what?" I asked, confused.

"Ask me," he said, placing his glass carefully on the table and folding his hands together in front of himself.

"Ask WHAT?" I said, not bothering to hide my annoyance.

"You *know* what. Just ask."

I paused a breath. I did know.

"Have I sold my soul?" I blurted out. I hadn't even allowed myself to formulate that as a coherent thought in my mind until I said it there at that table.

"Is that how I've *paid* for all this? Have I?"

Juan knelt up on his seat and spread his arms to 'Sin City' laid out before him, drawing glares from the family in the next booth.

"Would it matter if you *had* Mike? *Marcus*. This place is your playground. This place and everywhere beyond it!" He whirled his arms around, drawing more glares from the next table.

I had absolutely no idea how to answer that question. Until yesterday, I had never believed in 'Souls', good and evil, Heaven and Hell, Angels and Demons and all that bollocks. I still wasn't even sure that's what all this was.

I mirrored Juan by looking out to the neon view. All the possibilities laid out before me. Infinite opportunities beyond the desert in every direction. Happiness, fulfilment, validation, worth, excitement, all within touching distance for me now.

"Of course, it matters," I eventually replied.

"How can I enjoy this if the price is something terrible and this is something I regret. Forever… literally," I added.

Juan dropped back into his seat and faced me square on, although not before poking his tongue out at the sour-faced woman still staring and shaking her head in the next booth.

"Don't think of it like that," he started. "One way or the other people get what they deserve. You don't always see it but they do. 'Bad' people might sometimes seem to have good things happen to them, money, fame or whatever, but they are paying for it somewhere.

"In their quiet times. In their hearts or minds. In their reflections at the end of their day. Of their *days*. 'Good' people will sometimes appear to go unrewarded for their generosity, selflessness, kindness and often they are, not in 'things', not in 'stuff' but they are buying something *else* with that investment.

"What you purchase in your time here, Mike, is memories. Memories and love. Your own and peoples *of* you. It's unavoidable. We all pay our debt one way or the other. You and I will be no different."

I wasn't sure this completely answered my question. Or maybe it did. I tried to take in everything Juan had said. Was he saying I 'would' pay for all this or I wouldn't? Was there anything I could do about it now anyway? Would I take my old life back either way?

"Right!" he started again, rubbing his hands together and surveying the room.

"That guy there," he pointed to a man sitting holding court in a roped-off area with 'friends' sat either side, hanging off his every unnecessarily loud, word.

"Multi-millionaire, two houses in the Bahamas, a garage full of Sports Cars and a supermodel trophy wife. Makes his money selling life-saving drugs at inflated prices to underdeveloped countries. Super model trophy wife is banging her high school sweetheart whenever he's out of town, those 'friends' are only there because he's paying for everything and in twenty-two years, three months, five days, two hours and…"

Juan tapped on his watchless wrist. "Twenty-seven minutes…. He'll receive some data on an email explaining that if his company had reduced the cost of their miracle drug by just a few Cents, it could have saved another thirteen thousand lives. Men, Women and Children.

"Having known something like that was true for three decades, will already have him sleeping for a couple of hours a night at best, even before the clever science guys confirmed it with cold, hard facts. He'll see the faces of the people he could have saved eleven minutes later when he blows his brains out in his favourite Bentley."

"Bloody hell! Is that supposed to make me feel better? I feel like blowing my OWN brains out!"

Juan continued to look around the room, lips pursed, eyes darting.

"Her!" he suddenly squealed, pointing unsubtly to a waitress serving drinks to a table in a far corner. "Married in her twenties to the love of her life, widowed after a car accident five months later."

"OK, hang on!" I interrupted. "If you are trying to get me to hurl myself through this window and end it all on the pavement there next to that hot dog stand, you are doing a great job…I bet you're great fun at dinner parties!"

"Wait," he said. "I haven't finished. She left her home country to travel the world, which, admittedly, is something they had always planned to do together. She works two jobs to pay for her keep and travel and spends the rest of the time helping wherever will have her in the local communities she lands in. One day, she'll find love again, raise a family and see out many, many, *many* days more content than most people could ever dream of. Bloated and rich in the memories of the things she did."

I looked at the tired waitress as she smiled at a table beckoning her over to order their food. I turned towards the other VIP area and saw the Millionaire and his cronies guffawing at something he'd just said behind a wall of Champagne ice buckets and oversized bottles of premium vodka. How many of us would choose to be the waitress over the Pharma King given the choice?

It occurred to me that Juan could have just picked two random people from the restaurant and made-up stories about them but looking at the two subjects in question, something told me he hadn't.

"You'll get what you deserve, of that you can be sure," Juan said, beckoning over the waitress with a huge grin and exaggerated wave.

Obviously coming from him that was an ominous thing to hear and, I realised, could be taken either way.

"Great," I replied sarcastically, instantly feeling the need to drain a Mojito or seven myself.

"Let's get shots!" Blurted Juan suddenly, both reading my mind and lightening the mood. "You get them, I'm popping to the little boy's room," he said, sliding out of our booth. As he hurried past 'Sour Face's' table, I saw him silently click the fingers on his right hand.

Her large diet Coke instantly upended into her lap causing a scrabble for napkins and some language her husband had to apologise to their kids for. With his back to me, I couldn't see Juan's grin but knew it was there.

I wasn't certain if his stories were a pep talk or a warning. Perhaps they were both.

Some shots of something disgustingly strong and that tasted like crap, sounded perfect.

The waitress arrived with the same sincere smile I'd seen her give to half a dozen other customers whilst we'd been sitting there. She was taller than the other waitresses, lithe and toned, obviously from working two jobs where she was on her feet all day. I guessed at the early thirties which put her as older than most of the other table staff. Dark hair sprouted from a badly tied ponytail although it was likely to perfect when her shift started, God knows how long ago.

She did look tired, even more, so close up, but whether it was from the gruelling shift, the two jobs, the volunteering or simply wearing her story in her face, was impossible to tell. It made her no less pretty, however, and I realised I instinctively sucked my stomach in as she approached. Not that my new abs needed any assistance.

"Hi, my name is Jo, what can I get you guys?"

Chapter 7

"Oh, you're English?" I exclaimed with raised eyebrows and a disappointingly high-pitched tone.

"I am, and I'm guessing you are too then?" she replied with a warm expression it was impossible not to be drawn to.

What quickly then became apparent to me was that Marcus Taylor was equally lacking in 'cool' as Mike Barnes had spent 38 years being. No amount of money, body sculpting and chest hair would change that, and whilst looking for a witty and disarming reply, all I managed to do was make the pause long enough to make us both uncomfortable.

"Yes, yes, I am," I eventually managed to force out as if language was a new skill I had recently acquired.

Another painful silence was mercifully broken by her.

"…annnnd presumably you'd like to order some drinks?" she said mimicking an adult trying to guide a young child through some sort of complex maths problem.

"Yes, yes I would. Of course, I would. That's why we called you over. To order drinks. For us. To drink."

'Dick head', I thought, face-palming myself in my own mind.

"Splendid," she chirped. "That's what I'm here for, what can I getcha?"

"Shots," I managed to reply. "We want a round of shots. Something expensive that I won't ever remember drinking and strong enough to forget how badly I handled this conversation with you. If you please?"

Jo laughed and visibly relaxed. Perhaps relieved that she wasn't to be serving drinks to a complete imbecile all evening or possibly to share a rare moment of humour with a fellow Countryman.

"Hmmm," she pondered, tapping her pen on her perfect chin. "Leave it to me."

She turned and hurried towards the bar area. I instantly felt sad that she had gone. What the Hell was all that about? Get a grip on yourself man.

Halfway across the restaurant, Juan almost bumped into her on his way back from the Gents.

"She's even fitter close up," he said whilst shoving some complimentary crisps into his face and nodding towards Jo at the bar.

"Yeah? Can't say I noticed. Maybe yeah. S'pose."

Juan had stopped chewing mid-mouthful. Crumbs sat on his lips and most of his face. A rueful grin started to break across his mouth exposing the crisp mush inside as he watched me trying to look nonplussed. I ignored his stare for a few seconds, supposedly distracted by something on the street below. Eventually, I gave in and flicked a look at him. His annoying face beamed back at me.

"What?" I said.

"Nothing," he mumbled through the mouthful of crisps, which actually came out as '*muffen*'.

"Good," I said, going back to the important business of looking out of the window. Still, he maintained his childish smile while slowly recommencing his masticating.

"Fuck off," I said. "And if you wink at me, I'm putting you through this bloody great pane of glass."

Jo returned a few minutes later with some lethal-looking multicoloured liquid in shot glasses. I held up my hand as she started to describe to us what we were about to consume.

"I'll stop you there," I said. "I don't want to know," before grabbing it up, slamming it back and completing the process with a coughing fit.

All that Sin City had to offer potentially awaited me, but I was perfectly content to sit and get blind drunk in the same restaurant being served by the pretty Waitress. It had been a long and eventful day, to say the least. A pang of guilt that I had not made the most of my first twenty hours as Marcus Taylor, world's wealthiest man, did rear its head occasionally but was easily tamed by another shot of whatever it was we were drinking.

Every couple of rounds would be disappointingly brought to our table by another server but Jo's visits with pad and pen, or tray and drinks, were punctuated with some increasingly slurred, far from hilarious, one-liners from me. All of which she had likely heard before and all of which she laughed graciously at.

I managed to put up some token protestations when Juan eventually paid the bill, hoicked me under the armpit and lifted me, dead weight, out of the restaurant. A Limo was waiting on the street outside and within minutes I was slumped fully clothed, on the bed in my suite.

I awoke the next morning closer to lunchtime than breakfast. I'd managed to remove one shoe at some point in the night and some of the buttons on my shirt were open whilst others were missing entirely. I felt disappointed as I'd liked the shirt. Perhaps I'd buy another. Or twelve.

I tried to recall the last part of the evening as I scrabbled for the bottle of water on the bedside table. It felt like the elixir of life as it slid down my parched throat.

A wave of shame came crashing in as I remembered my unceremonious exit from the fake Eiffel Tower.

The short walk to the shower looked like an epic cross-continent adventure from where I was sprawled, but, as I managed to raise my head for another swig of the water, I spotted what looked like a note, stuck on a dressing table mirror. Intrigued, I fought back nausea and swung myself off the bed. As I approached the mirror and my own reflection came into view, I jumped and stumbled back, still not used to seeing a different me staring back.

My shins crashed into the edge of a glass table flipping it over and as momentum threw me forward over the table, I promptly threw up. Last night's mystery shots exploded onto the glass table and marble floor, accompanied by their best friends Mr Buffalo wings and Mrs Cheesy Fries.

Once I was certain my shame was complete, I wiped my mouth on the sleeve of my busted shirt and finished what was left of the water.

Being extra especially careful not to tread in last night's consumptions with the foot without a shoe, I started my epic journey again.

It was a note on the mirror:

Morning Marcus!

Drink plenty of water and mind the table in the middle of the floor!

You won't see me for a while now, your induction is over, you're on your own, Boss!

The world is your oyster but doesn't forget the 'Laws'!

1. You can't tell anyone! ANYTHING!
2. You can't contact anyone you knew in a previous 'life'.
3. You can't give life-changing amounts of money to anyone. NO MATTER WHAT!
4. You only get another 364 days as Marcus Taylor, DON'T WASTE IT!
5. There are consequences to breaking ANY of the above!

Good Luck!
Juan

P.S. and this is the last time I clean up for you! ;)

I held the note and read it over and over. Eventually, as I was making another run through the scrawled letter from Juan, there was a heat in my fingers, and I was forced to drop it onto the dresser. With an intense flash, an unnatural, tall, thin, Serpent like flame shot up from the paper.

And it was gone. Not a trace it had ever existed. No ash, no corner of the note left wilted on the dresser. No burn mark on the dresser top. Gone.

I turned back towards the room which was now immaculately put together. Glass table back on its four legs and no evidence of the previous evening splattered across it, or the floor. The bed was pristine and appeared unslept on, and I was aware that my mouth no longer felt like it was made of chipboard.

As I stood and began to consider the possibilities of the day ahead, a ray of sun came through the window and bounced off the face of my watch, causing me to flinch away from it. Looking back at the watch, I noticed a new counter underneath the *'El Diablo'* logo. It had three tiny dials and as I considered what I was seeing, they ticked over from,

'*3 6 5*'.

to

'*3 6 4*'.

One day is done.

Chapter 8

I bounced through the lobby of the hotel with a new zest for life. Where yesterday had been tinged with disbelief, apprehension, and uncertainty, today felt like the dawning of something exciting, plump, and heavy with untold prospects and anticipation. That I had possibly sold my soul, was likely damned to spend eternity getting buggered senseless by the guy from the 'go compare' adverts and my only 'friend' was an annoying, magicy Demon type thing that used to clean pools for me, didn't seem to matter today.

'*Carpe Diem*' I thought, as I stepped out into the searing Nevadan heat.

I made a beeline for 'Caesars Palace' and spent countless hours on high stakes Roulette tables, sharing wins and losses with some of the wealthiest people in the world. Champagne glasses were clinked with people whose faces I recognised but couldn't always place, particularly behind oversized sunglasses or under designer baseball caps. Rappers with an entourage the size of an army, ageing actresses with twenty-one-year-old boyfriends and Sports Stars impressing a gallery of beautiful and expectant gold diggers with stories of championship wins.

Invites to pool parties and after-show 'get togethers' filled my diary by the evening. It turned out that a 'down-to-Earth' Millionaire from somewhere in England nobody had ever heard of, could be quite the hit in Sin City.

During a game of Poker for which the 'buy-in' was an eye-watering $50,000 just to get you started, I found myself seated next to a tall, black guy who, it turned out, was a Basketball player for the local franchise team. He was being traded to another team in New York and was having a party at his home that evening where the great and beautiful of Las Vegas would be gathering to bid him farewell.

During a failed attempt to explain the offside rule in 'Soccer' to him, he invited me to his party. Not just due to my compelling company and sparkling wit but because, during a particularly enjoyable winning streak on a Roulette table earlier, I had shouted for the entire Casino's benefit, "I'm never leaving this place!" followed by a highly uncharacteristic "Wahoooo!"

Although partly induced by free champagne, this swiftly began to form into the idea of buying a property in Vegas sooner rather than later. Because why not?

Deonte, the basketball player was selling his eight-bedroom Super home, complete with swimming pools (plural), cinema room, bowling alley and its own nightclub, and he felt I should consider buying it from him. He did look confused when I drunkenly put my arm around him and demanded 'mate's rates' but I guess some things don't translate from English to American that well.

I showered and changed in a vague attempt to sober up before heading off to an address scribbled on the back of a Caesars Palace drinks coaster. My main focus for the evening was to try and not make a dick of myself in front of some of Vegas's most influential and regarded people.

Basketball dude had mumbled through a list of guests I could expect to see later and it included two actors from a film I'd watched last week (I hoped they wouldn't ask me what I thought of it as I'd fallen asleep through the second half), a popstar whose latest CD was rattling around in the glove box of my Fiat 500 back in Spain and a famous comedian of whom I'd watched everything they'd ever done.

The chances of maintaining a reasonable level of 'cool' were already poor to none, without me rocking up pissed. I chain drank two coffees before checking the hair and heading out.

On reflection, I don't recall how big I imagined the house to be before I arrived, but it was bigger than that. Much bigger.

As you stepped out of your car next to the giant fountain roundabout on arrival, you were forced to turn your head as if you were watching a tennis match to look along its width and see both ends.

It was a monolith of a building in a mock Georgian style. Although it flirted with tacky, it was impossible not to be impressed by its grandeur. Perfectly manicured and landscaped gardens had been designed to sweep the visitor towards imposing double front doors flanked with ornate pillars and topiary trees taller than the house's owner.

As my cab pulled away and crunched back down the gravel driveway, I couldn't help but imagine what cars I could put in the quadruple garage, also mock Georgian, far off to my right, set amongst some taller trees. Parked around the roundabout fountain were guests' exuberant vehicles. A yellow and red Ferrari, a gold-plated Lamborghini, a Hummer with crystal-encrusted wheels and a Rolls Royce which had been custom stretched to include a jacuzzi where the boot should be. I couldn't help but wonder where he put his shopping.

Before I could ring the fist-sized doorbell, the door was opened by an attractive young blonde lady wearing black heels, black fishnet tights, black hot pants and a white shirt which looked like it needed to be another two sizes larger to even begin to contain her considerable assets.

She stood aside with a welcoming and disarming smile, and I stepped into what I had already decided was to be my new home.

"Good evening, sir," she said in a Southern drawl, motioning me towards a table containing endless rows of champagne. As I helped myself, It did occur to me that I might need to hydrate myself with something other than champagne and coffee at some point in the near future.

Music thumped through the house but seemed to be originating from the back of the Mansion where I guessed the main pool and hub of the party was already going strong. I passed all sorts of groups of intimidatingly glamorous people as I made my way back and suddenly wished I hadn't been quite so effective in my attempts to sober up. I drained my glass and swapped it for a fresh glass from another provocatively dressed server making rounds.

I left the relative safety of the house and stepped out into the rear gardens of the property. There remained plenty of heat in the evening, despite it pushing nine p.m. and I had to shield my eyes from the sun, yet to completely set behind the mountains in the distance.

"Shoelace dude!" A familiar voice bellowed across the lake sized swimming pool and, as is now apparent, I'd decided to embrace the absurdity of Juan's cover story about how my wealth had been generated.

I made my way around the pool towards my new friend and, by their size, what looked to be three of his teammates. I was probably coming in at somewhere around six feet tall but felt like Frodo amongst his travelling companions, as greetings were exchanged.

I managed to keep my fascinating and completely fictitious explanation of the nuances of the shoelace industry to a minimum but still a few seconds longer than it managed to hold everyone's attention.

Very quickly the conversation got back to Basketball contracts and so I mumbled, "Gonna grab another drink," and slinked away.

I saw the famous actors he'd mentioned sitting sharing a sunbed and sipping cocktails, one of the three Swans hired to float around in the pool, craning its neck to eat the crumbs they were dropping from a bowl of crisps.

I was making my way towards a marquee that was being used as a pop-up bar when I saw the comedian, a genuine hero of mine, engrossed in what appeared to be a deep and meaningful conversation with a woman half his age and of whom he had a handful of her left breast. He was, what can only be described as 'jiggling' it.

I decided to try and have a chat with him later.

I zig-zagged through small groups of beautiful people, some natural, some clearly not so much, and was grateful to reach the shade of the marquee.

Resting my elbows on the bar, I looked at the overwhelming selection of drinks bottles laid out on the table behind it. Water. I just wanted water.

"You look better than you did when your mate carried you home last night."

Jo, the waitress from the 'Paris' restaurant, was behind the bar, drying a glass with a small towel. She was smiling the way your mum would look at you if you'd done something naughty, but funny. One eyebrow raised; chin dipped slightly. Stood there. Being all perfect and lovely. And did I mention perfect?

"Wow, hi!" I bumbled. "What are you doing here? Sorry. Stupid question, working behind the bar. Clearly. That's obvious. Because you are behind the bar. Working."

'Smooth' I thought to myself with another mental facepalm.

Jo nodded slowly and condescendingly, maintaining the smile.

She was even more lovely than I remembered her from the night before. Not because her perfect hair had been more carefully prepared or the tightness of the clothing against her perfect shape but because, in the daylight, I could see simply see her properly. She had one of those faces that would have fitted right in on the other side of the bar, schmoozing with the models and film stars but wouldn't have seemed out of place in a queue for the deli counter at Tesco.

"Of course!" I continued "You work two jobs. This is the other one."

"How do you know I work two jobs?" She said scowling.

"You told me last night. Didn't you?"

"Nope, pretty sure I didn't," she said with an accusing stare.

Juan had told me when he first spoke about her. Shit.

"Yeah, you mentioned you were from England and had to work two jobs to pay for your travel. I remember now, it was when you brought us our third lot of buffalo wings. Yep, that's right."

Jo looked doubtful but seemed to accept the explanation enough to move on, the thought that I was some sort of stalker clearly lurked, however.

I waved a 'you go ahead' to a glamorous looking woman who arrived at the bar to order a vodka martini.

Jo brought me water with a disappointed expression that screamed 'lightweight' and I sipped it whilst feeling the throb of the bass from the music system coming up through my feet.

I felt completely out of my depth again as I leaned against the bar and observed the throng of people, all of whom were very clearly enjoying the party more than I was.

"So, shoelaces then?"

Jo was back with another towel and another glass.

"Shoelaces," I nodded.

"Can't believe there'd be that much money in *shoelaces*?"

"Oh, there is. Imagine a world without shoelaces. Peoples shoes fall off all the time, accidents left, right and centre. It would be chaos. I'm almost singlehandedly responsible for keeping the world on its feet."

"I'd never looked at it like that," Jo said sarcastically while dropping ice into a glass for a guy so tall he had to bend to get into the marquee.

A booming voice over the PA system announced the evening's main entertainment was about to begin on a makeshift stage that had been erected on a vast lawn behind the tent I was in. After a brief rush for drinks, the marquee was empty again but for Jo, two other bar staff and me. I decided to remain in the tent despite hearing the muffled intro to one of the summer's biggest tunes being performed by a multi-Grammy winner on the stage behind me.

"You not going? I hear he's great live," Jo asked, ambling over to the section of a bar I was standing in.

"Not really my cup of tea," I lied, curling my nose up and taking another sip of water.

While she answered my questions about how she had ended up in Vegas, things she'd seen since she'd been there and some of the other places she had travelled to, I worked hard to avoid any questions I would struggle to give a truthful answer to. Which was really restricting. She laughed at an abridged version of my story of stumbling around in my room hungover, smashing into the table and throwing up, and she regaled me with tales of badly behaved household names who had visited the restaurant.

It turned out we had grown up not a million miles apart, in an area of South East England west of London and had even been to some of the same places. I had tears streaming down my face as we retold stories of a club we had both visited in our youth, a grotty meat market of sticky floors and underage drinking.

"I'm Jo, by the way," she said, dropping a towel onto the bar and thrusting out her right hand. "Not sure if your memory of last night stretched that far?"

"I was still compos mentis at that stage, don't worry," I replied with a grin.

"Mike," I said in return, touching her hand for the first time. "Marcus. I mean Marcus."

Christ. Way to go.

"Mike Marcus?" Jo said with a puzzled expression.

"No. Not Mike Marcus. Not Mike. Just Marcus. Look," I said fumbling my credit card out of my pocket and holding it up as evidence.

'Well-handled knob head' I thought, berating myself again.

"Okayyyyy…" she said, clearly concerned that that guy she was talking to, wasn't sure of his own name.

"Yeah, Mike's my middle name. Some members of my family call me by that. It was my grandad's name." Partly true. Decent recovery.

"Anyway," I said, moving on. "Nice to meet you, Jo."

"Nice to meet you too, not Mike."

She laughed again, and I forced a fake one.

The evening wore on and between her serving the occasional Porn Star Martini, we giggled and bitched our way through old relationship war stories, jobs we'd had and stupid things we'd done as kids. Still, she hadn't mentioned the fact that she had lost her husband, and it was niggling away at the fringes of the conversation at times. Still, she'd known me a matter of hours and it was her business.

By this stage I was back drinking my way through the array of alcoholic beverages lined up in front of me and Jo had secreted a glass of wine under the bar next to where I was stood, chatting to me and taking sips when the bar supervisor was distracted. How are all millionaires not alcoholics? I asked myself. Perhaps they were.

I was mustering the courage to chuck in a "Wanna grab a drink when you get off?" when I suddenly felt a hand slap my right butt cheek.

"Hey, lover boy, I didn't know you knew Deonte?"

Raquel, the woman from the blackjack table whom I'd got to know *extremely* well yesterday afternoon, had appeared next to me at the bar and was now stroking my right arm.

"Hi you, yeah, no I don't really, we met at Caesars earlier, and he kindly invited me along. Great party, eh?" I was aware that Jo was still standing with us and had clocked the arm stroking. I pulled away to grab a drink stirrer I didn't need.

"Yeah, grrrreat party," Raquel slurred.

"Not as good as our little private party in your suite yesterday though," she said with a wink.

A lead weight formed in my stomach as I watched Jo awkwardly drift away to the other end of the bar.

"When are we going for round two?" Raquel said, trying and failing to lean seductively against the bar. The combination of ludicrously high heeled stilettos and alcohol got the better of her.

I wanted the Earth to swallow me up.

I managed to manoeuvre the conversation to other topics until Raquel introduced me to some acquaintances who had come looking for the drinks she was obviously supposed to be fetching.

Eventually, she was dragged away, back to the bedlam of the party on the lawn, but not before she'd made me promise to find her later.

I hated how that must have sounded to Jo, what she must think of me, and the lead weight in my stomach refused to budge.

I tried in vain to grab Jo's attention, to use my newly acquired gift for twisting the truth and have her not think whatever she was thinking. She was suddenly, constantly busy with wiping surfaces or glass collecting or serving party goers. I knew how I looked. Another rich guy in Vegas, out for one thing. She'd seen my type a thousand times, of that I was sure.

No matter how I manoeuvred myself up and down the bar, Jo always seemed to be somewhere else.

A little while later I spotted her saying something to her supervisor before taking off her apron and disappearing through a gap in the back of the tent, obviously on a break.

I felt sick to the stomach. Not due to the Pina Coladas I'd been sinking or the mountain of seafood canapes I'd been working my through but because, firstly, she felt like the only, flimsy, connection to my old life and secondly, because I really liked her. I really liked her, and she obviously thought I was a bit of a knob. I hated that. I'd always hated people thinking poorly of me, even when I deserved it.

I decided I was going to stride up to her and make her understand. Make her see that I'm an alright guy. I wasn't in Vegas shagging everything that moved, it had been a one-off in a strange and stressful day. It wasn't easy being a newly reborn trillionaire. I would explain that to her.

Maybe without the 'trillionaire' bit.

I noticed I'd go through another Pina Colada and a handful of Chilli and Prawn skewers, and yet Jo hadn't returned from her break. I called another one of the servers across.

"Yes, sir?" said a young, friendly looking, Hispanic guy.

"I'll have another one of these please," I said rattling the multiple straws, cocktail umbrella, and fake parrot, in my glass.

"No problem," the barman said, *almost* managing to hide his judgement of my choice of drink. He returned with my cocktail a few moments later, and I couldn't see the surface of the drink for all of the cocktail paraphernalia he'd arranged in it.

'Cheeky bugger' I thought to myself, taking a long indignant suck on one of the four pink straws.

"Anything else, sir," he said with a hint of sarcasm that there is a reasonable chance I imagined.

"Yeah, actually, there is, Jo, the girl that's been serving me all night, she's been on her break a long time? I said I'd help her with…err, with something. Any idea how long she'll be?"

The young guy looked sceptical but walked the length of the bar, said something to the supervisor and ambled back.

"She's not on a break. Her shift finished; she was just covering for a few hours. She's gone home."

Frustration was probably the main feeling I was left with. Frustration that I hadn't had the chance to explain. Let her see the *real* me.

I consoled myself by draining the cocktail and ordering another. Carrying my drink outside, I did a quick shimmy

94

and duck behind an ice sculpture that the Basketball player had apparently commissioned of himself, to avoid Raquel who was propping herself up on two friends.

"Hey man!" It was confusing as I initially thought the sculpture had spoken to me, but it was Deonte himself appearing from behind the tent.

"What do you think of my little crib?" he said slapping a huge arm around me and turning me to look at the behemoth of a house before us.

"It's really nice. Amazing. I imagine you'll miss it?"

"I can always come and visit it when it's yours, Marcus!" he said chuckling, and nearly squeezing all the breath from my lungs.

I looked again at the house, this time from the rear. You could have comfortably housed ten families in it. I'd only ever seen houses like this on TV. From the first floor, you'd be able to see the Las Vegas Strip to the front and beyond a line of Palm Trees at the rear of the property, the sun rising and setting beyond the mountains.

The sun had now dipped behind the horizon, setting the Nevada sky ablaze with reds, oranges and purples.

It was the biggest sky I had ever seen.

"Yeah, why not," I said. "I'll take it."

Chapter 9

A month had passed since I'd moved into my new home. Those weeks had gone by in a blur of gambling, partying, eating, drinking, and floating around on my pool on a giant Lilo. I was in serious danger of turning my new body into my old body.

I had a full-time cook, a housemaid and a full-time housekeeper/assistant, all of whom had come as part of the package when I bought the house.

Although I had thoroughly enjoyed four weeks of flat-out hedonistic pleasure, thoughts of Jo would inevitably creep in and spoil my mood. I also knew full well that it wasn't sustainable and at some point, I would need to sort myself out or risk dying of exposure or starvation, having got too big to disembark my own Lilo.

Invites to soirees and after-show parties were easy to come by in the predominantly superficial world of the Las Vegas high roller. That was me now. From Deputy Assistant Manager at a packaging company in High Wycombe to 'High Roller and friend to the Stars'. Fuck you, Bill.

It wasn't all boozing and gambling and (almost always) turning down one-night stands with gold diggers. I met some genuinely interesting and good-hearted people, people who were using a good chunk of their wealth to benefit others and it always pulled at somewhere inside me that I was prevented from doing the same by the 'Laws'. I would have to make myself feel better by buying something shiny, fast, or huge. I'd won a yacht from a German businessman in a game of poker one evening back at the Palazzo and it was moored up in a Marina in LA.

Two weeks later, I still didn't have any plans to go and see it. I kept thinking that I was wasting the resources at my disposal, that I should jump on a plane and see the world, have some adventures, meet different people, but then I'd generally put my feet up in front of my hundred-inch TV and promise myself I'd look at it again tomorrow. I also kept a feeling that perhaps I'd run into Jo again and she'd fall madly in love with me.

It seemed like whenever I went back to 'Paris' to find her, to explain to her, it was never her shift or she was off sick, or had a few days off. I started to suspect she had told colleagues to fob me off if I came in looking for her.

Other than the pining for a woman I hardly knew, I was enjoying life too much to bother going anywhere else. I'd already experienced the attention you receive from beautiful women when you pull up at an exclusive nightclub in a quarter-million-dollar Ferrari. It was a hard thing to move on from.

I made a compromise with myself. I'd stay in Vegas for the time being but improve my lifestyle. A bit.

I was recommended a personal trainer, an ex-Navy Seal who would arrive at my house and to whom I would pay $200 an hour to make me wish I were dead. Money well spent.

I bought some shares in the local Basketball team through a guy Deonte had introduced me to, and that became my hobby. I'd go to the games, meet up with other members of the board, get invited on fishing trips, rounds of golf and the occasional 'gentleman's evening'. Ever tried playing golf, or any sport for that matter, with someone else's arms? Not easy. They stopped inviting me after I nearly killed the owner of the New York Nicks by badly slicing a ball off the fourth tee.

I also ticked off one of the items on the pathetic list I'd written on my first day as Marcus Taylor and bought a guitar. It had belonged to Eric Clapton and had later been bought by some scrawny looking guitarist from a band I'd never heard of but who was supposedly very popular amongst the younger population. He was twenty-two and owned a house equally as big as mine, in the same gated development I lived in. The guitar cost me the same as my first house in Wycombe.

I found a guitar tutor online and despite some mild halitosis, he did know his stuff. I had an hour a day with him for the next four weeks in between practising myself when not too hungover. After that, we would get together once a week so he could give me a few pointers. It reached the stage where I was confident playing a few songs in the company of friends if the party ended up back at my place. And I'd drunk enough to overcome the stage fright.

I continued to eyeball the catering staff at house parties and events in the hope of spotting Jo. Would she even remember me? Why did I care this much?

For all, I knew she'd saved enough money and moved on to the next adventure. Obviously wasn't meant to be.

Life was good and, it's fair to say, everything you would imagine it would be. I can't sit here and say it was empty, meaningless, shallow and void of genuine connections because it just didn't feel like that at the time. It felt like an endless vacation with no limitations as to the possibilities. I was quite literally living the dream.

I had no restraints on my movements or what I did with the hours in the day, had some good friends from the time I did spend at the Basketball and couldn't think of much I would have changed. Eventually, once I'd given up on finding and reconciling with Jo, I even started seeing a woman ten years younger than me whom I'd met the very same day that I'd seen her in a five-storey high Ralph Lauren advert on the side of a Hotel.

Sometimes, however, back at home, after the roulette wheels had stopped turning and the pavements were more street cleaners than gamblers, it was impossible not to consider the absurdity of my new life.

In amongst the relentless pleasure-seeking that had defined the first few weeks and months, it had still been a confusing blur of trying to come to terms with my reality. I'd had to embrace the incomprehensible amount of cash I had and learn to deal with the pressures and trappings that brought with it. Everyone wanted to be your best friend, and I was grateful this was happening to me as I approached forty and not in my twenties.

I felt sympathy for the sports and rock stars who find themselves in this Universe without the perspective and wisdom that age itself brings. I pondered this while sitting alone at home in my enormous house supping imported lager. I felt wise and worthy. Like a good looking, rich, Yoda.

It took me a surprisingly short amount of time to feel at home in my new body (except when playing golf), perhaps because it was so much better than the old one.

Of course, there were people I missed, even people I didn't think I would. Not enough to do anything about it though.

Six months since Marcus had burst into existence was coming round fast.

I decided to mark the occasion with a party to end all parties at one of the most exclusive venues in Vegas. A rooftop club in the heart of the Strip.

I invited everyone I'd met since arriving. The entire Basketball team were there, every high roller in Vegas got an invite, models, TV personalities, global sports stars, politicians, anyone I'd spent any time with at the tables in those six months.

The evening was perfect. I'd dressed it up as being my Birthday, seeing as nobody knew when my birthday was. As I greeted my guests, I was lavished with gifts of jewellery, paintings, sculptures and even a Black Panther kitten that I had no idea what to do with.

Nadine, my supermodel booty call, was dressed in a little black number that had less material than some pairs of Y-fronts I owned and was getting plenty of looks from both male and female guests.

As I took a glass of champagne from a passing silver tray, something occurred to me.

It was Friday.

Quiz night at Churchill's.

Gary would be arguing with one of the regulars about whether the Vatican is a Country or a City and Linda would be getting drooled on by the old perverts at the bar and likely loving every second of it.

I stood and let the music wash over me for a moment. A cool breeze was making an otherwise hot Vegas evening, bearable.

It had been the most ridiculous, incredible, unbelievable, mind-blowing six months. So many people. So many nights. So many things. I'm not sure I would have changed much.

Maybe one thing.

"Can I take your glass, sir?" a voice asked from behind me. A voice I had heard before.

I turned. Jo was standing in waitress uniform holding a tray of empty champagne glasses. A loose strand of her hair was being blown about her face by the breeze, and she swept it back up with the hand not holding the tray. At that moment, it was the simplest but most elegant thing I'd ever seen.

Nobody would have said she was prettier, sexier, than the woman I'd arrived at the party with, but there was an irresistible *gravity* to her that instantly pulled me in like the first time at the restaurant and then at Deonte's party. I went from being the confident and enigmatic host, comfortable amongst the great and the good to feeling about fourteen years old.

"Hey! You are still here; in Vegas I mean? I've been back to the restaurant a few times but never caught you there?"

Jo looked genuinely happy to see me and beamed a smile back. In that instant, it was possibly the happiest and most relieved I had ever felt.

"Wow, it's been a little while…" she clearly couldn't recall my name. Why would she?

"Marcus," I said.

"…Marcus, that's right I remember now. Shoelaces, right?" she said pointing down at my thousand-dollar shoes. That, ironically, were slip-ons.

"Shoelaces," I nodded. "And it's been almost exactly six months. I thought you'd moved on to bigger and better things?"

"Nope still here, we are building a centre for underprivileged kids up in the old town, and I promised I'd hang around until it's done. I was an architect in a previous life so I'm kind of trying to keep it all going in the right direction for them. Nearly done though."

I felt my heart sink.

"How long before it's finished?" I said, trying to sound nonchalant.

"Few months, hopefully, it will be ready for Christmas."

"OK, Christmas. Ages away. Plenty of time," I thought to myself.

"Anyway, nice to see you again," she said, lowering the tray for me to place my now empty glass on. She leaned in and spoke from behind her hand "I'd better crack on, apparently the guy whose party it is can be a bit of a dick."

I stared at her and raised one eyebrow.

She stared back briefly with a confused expression, that became realisation, that became an embarrassment.

"Oh, my God, I'm so sorry! It's your party, isn't it? Isn't it? I'm such an idiot, it was just one of the other waitresses, something about a tip you took back after you'd already given it? Your money, do what you like I say," she said finishing with a nervous laugh.

A month or so ago I had been completely wasted in this very bar. At the end of the evening, I paid the bill and, being in a jolly and generous mood, threw a $10,000 tip on the table. It was only as I made my way to the elevator it dawned me like being hit on the head with a sledgehammer that: '*you can't give away life-changing amounts of money*'.

I had to race back to the table and wrestle the tip out of the waitress's hand, quickly deciding that $565 wasn't going to change anyone's life and thrusting notes to that value back into her hand before turning tail. Not my finest hour.

"Yeah, it was dickish," I went on to explain. "I was really drunk and forgot that it was my friend's money I'd been looking after. Got a bit carried away, nearly gave his 10 G's away!"

The whole thing sounded ridiculous as it came out of my mouth, but it was the best I could come up with at the time.

"I'm still sorry," Jo said, her face just as perfect when scarlet with embarrassment.

"Honestly don't worry, It's not the first time I've been called a dick and won't be the last. Probably not the last time *tonight* to be fair, it's only 11 o'clock."

Jo laughed with relief and seemed to regain her composure.

She shuffled on her feet and straightened her skirt with her free hand.

"OK, I really had better collect up some glasses though, I could do without having to find another job."

"Wait. Just a second. Look, it's really nice to have someone to chat to that knows where you are from. I don't know if you agree? Anyway, any chance you fancy grabbing a coffee with me at some point? No pressure. No pressure... buuuut, if you say 'no' I'll have you fired and you'll lose your job and could end up on the street and while you are eating peoples rubbish from a dumpster you'll think 'why didn't I just have a coffee with that dick?'"

Watching Jo laugh made me the happiest man alive, and I made a mental note to try and make that happen as often as possible.

"What do you say?" I finished.

"Fine, but if you could keep the dickishness to a minimum that would be great?"

"Dickishness?" I asked.

"Dickishness," she said again.

"It's a word. Anyway, won't the face of Ralph Laurens winter collection mind?" Jo asked, nodding towards Nadine, who was surrounded by a group of posturing middle-aged men from the golf club, all of whom were married and all of whom regularly seemed to forget that fact.

"We are just company for each other while she's in town. The conversation isn't exactly riveting if I'm honest. Anyway, she flies out to Monaco in the morning for a shoot."

I wouldn't let Jo carry on with her work until she had typed her number into my phone, which she did with quick and nimble fingers and a guilty glance towards Nadine. I reassured her again that she wasn't my girlfriend and had nothing to worry about. I'm not completely sure Nadine would concur, but she *was* flying out tomorrow and potentially wouldn't be back for a couple of weeks.

I did feel slightly uncomfortable downplaying my relationship with Nadine, but there was no way I was letting Jo walk away without some reassurance and confidence I'd see her again.

Jo handed me back my phone, and I checked the number she had typed. It seemed like a legitimate number, the correct amount of digits etc and so I took that as a positive. I looked back at her before we both smiled and subtly nodded to each other. She took my empty glass from me, placed it on her tray and walked away without saying another word.

I watched her become part of the crowd as she weaved in and out of the throng of people. I waited, heart quickening like a teenager at a school disco.

And I waited.

She was getting further and further away and was becoming more and more obscured by the mass of guests.

And then there it was.

The look back.

A simple glance over her shoulder said everything and made me feel like the luckiest man on Earth. Even more than usual.

We met for coffee two days later at a traditional American 'Mom and Pop' diner just off the Strip. One coffee turned into two, turned into a brunch of waffles and maple syrup.

The six months since we'd spoken last melted away and we took each other back to the schools, streets, and homes of our childhoods.

We laughed at Christmas day family arguments, consoled at heart-breaking teenage breakups and winced at broken bones. We playfully argued over whose hometown was the biggest dump and eventually had to agree to disagree.

I'd covered off my, actual, extremely humble beginnings by explaining that I'd inherited the shoelace empire from a long-lost Uncle at some point in my thirties. She didn't question it, and I skirted around the subject where possible.

The attraction was obvious, our eyes would linger on each other a nanosecond too long and there was some subtle, and not so subtle, flirting from the first minute we'd sat down. She did remember Raquel interrupting our chat and admitted that she had felt disappointed as 'she did really like' me. Hearing her say that made my stomach flip, and I had to hide a grin behind my glass of Coke. '*Get a grip, Mike!*' I thought to myself.

Four hours was gone in the blink of an eye and Jo's impending shift at the 'Paris' Hotel began to loom like a heavy black cloud.

"Call in sick," I said, with no hint of irony. "Call in sick and we'll go somewhere else for a bite to eat and see where the day takes us."

"I can't do that, it's not fair, I'm supposed to be there in less than an hour. I couldn't, there'd be short-staffed. It's not fair."

I had already started to get an idea of how better a person she was than me and began to worry that it wouldn't be long before she worked that out. I had called in sick at my old job for all sorts of reasons. My poor old Nan had died on at least three occasions, my non-existent cat (I hate cats) once

106

swallowed a Duracell battery and had to be taken to the vets and if I called in with one more 'rare and potent strain of stomach flu' they would have sold me off to the pharmaceutical industry to study.

If I was a horse, they would have shot me. That any of this would potentially burden my work colleagues was never a consideration.

"I don't want to sound like some desperate saddo," I said. "But I've had my best morning for ages, haven't laughed like that since I don't know when. I just wondered when, you know, what time, if you wanted…"

"10 o'clock," Jo interrupted.

"10 o'clock what?" I said.

"You were going to ask me what time I got off. 10 o'clock. Meet me at the front of the hotel at quarter past."

I couldn't hide my joy that she wanted to see me again. I put my fork down on the plate of what remained of my waffles and sat back in my chair content and with a childish grin.

"Waste not, want not," Jo said, pulling my plate towards her and stabbing at my leftovers with the fork. They had disappeared before I'd even had time to object. All but some maple syrup on her chin.

"Lucky I like a woman with an appetite," I said, shaking my head in disbelief.

"You'd better!" she said sternly. "I plan on being enormous by the time I'm fifty. Best you get used to the idea now!"

Even joking about knowing each other at fifty gave me a feeling of warm contentedness. At that moment, I wanted it to be true more than anything in the world.

I had to promise I would let her pay the next bill to allow me to pay for this one before we walked out of the air-conditioned paradise of the diner and into the breath-taking heat of a Las Vegas September.

"I guess I'll see you tonight then," I said, as we stood on the shadeless pavement awkwardly, unsure of the appropriate way to end our date. If that's what it was.

"I guess you will," Jo said, before deciding for us both by putting her hand out in front for me to shake.

I took it firmly and exaggerated the formality by straightening my spine and pulling back my shoulders.

"Then I will bid you a good day," I said.

Jo smiled and nodded before flagging down a passing cab and climbing in. The car drove away but not before I'd got the look and wave I had hoped for.

I walked through the front doors of my home and it had never felt so empty. I tried to relax in the pool, shot some hoops on the bespoke basketball court Deonte had built and played some guitar, but it was still the longest eight hours of my life waiting to be able to see Jo again. I tried to kill some time chatting to Maria, my housekeeper, but she was coming to the end of her shift and did a very poor job of pretending to be interested in my plans for the Basketball team or what I was going to wear on my date that evening.

I had to send some texts to some acquaintances bailing from my weekly game of poker at Caesars Palace. They found it challenging hiding their disappointment. This wasn't due to the high quality of my company but had more to do with the low quality of my poker.

Some of these guys had bought third and fourth homes with the money I'd lost to them over the past few months.

I'd decided I needed to own a Lear Jet a few weeks previously and it was sat at the airstrip for one day before I lost it to a record producer on the turn of a card and never even got to see it. Easy come, easy go.

Having got ready, very slowly, I grabbed my car keys from a small electronically locked cupboard next to the front door which also contained the keys to five other vehicles gathering dust in the garage.

I pulled the front door open to head off.

"FOR FUCK' SAKE!" I screeched, stumbling backwards into my house.

"Hello, stranger!"

Juan was standing in my doorway in a fur coat that looked four sizes too big, a woollen bobble hat and snow boots.

It was still eighty degrees outside despite being almost ten o'clock at night.

"What are you doing here?" I said trying to compose myself "And what are you wearing?"

"Oh, this? Yeah, it was cold where I have just come from. We do feel the cold! Can I come in then?" he said, stepping past me regardless.

"I'm actually just going out, is it important?" I asked.

"From how far away do you think I've come? Yeah, it's important," Juan said, spreading his arms and inviting me to consider his clothing.

"Yeah, OK, fair enough, what's up?"

"I have been asked just to give you a little reminder of the 'Laws' my old friend. We can see where this is going with this 'Jo', and it's raising some concern at 'Head

Office', shall we say. Love can do some strange things to a man."

"Woooah!" I said, holding my hands up in front of me.

"Love? Love? I've only met her a couple of times!" I emphasised the ludicrousness of his statement by laughing far too hard and far too long.

Juan raised his eyebrows and stared at me with a concerned shake of the head.

"Mike," Juan started. I hadn't been called that name for so long, and I instinctively recoiled from it. Hearing it felt like it burst some sort of reality bubble I'd been existing in quite happily.

"I'm here just to say *BE CAREFUL*, you are on the run down to the end of your year as Marcus Taylor and then, as you well know, you won't be able to contact anyone from Marcus' life. Anyone."

I had successfully managed to force these facts, of which I was well aware, to the back of my mind since seeing Jo again. I felt deflated having been so high on nervous anticipation before opening the door to my house.

"I'll be fine," I lied. "I'll keep it casual. Breezy. I'm breezy!"

"Consequences Mike. Consequences."

And with that, Juan pulled his bobble hat further down over his ears, walked back past me, and out of the door, slamming it closed behind him. I rushed to the door and yanked it open less than a second after it had clicked shut.

"WHAT CONSEQUENCES?" I called to my huge deserted driveway. Juan was nowhere to be seen. He'd gone. Disappeared.

Water gurgled and bubbled in the illuminated fountain and ground-level lights threw shadows onto the manicured shrubs and trees. I stood motionless in the doorway and considered what he'd said. Perhaps he was right, and I was heading into something that could never have a happy ending.

We were both leaving Vegas at some point, ultimately this probably was a waste of time. Someone was going to get hurt if this went the way every fibre of my being wanted it to. A line from an old song popped into my head *'if I go there will be trouble, and if I stay there will be double!'* I remained in the doorway for another moment to try and make the right decision.

I closed the door.

And headed to my garage.

Chapter 10

For the next few months, Jo and I spent more and more time together, despite her refusing to take unauthorised leave from work and keeping both her jobs. We almost had our first major argument when I suggested she didn't need both sets of wages coming in as she could spend a certain amount of time at mine, and that I had plenty of everything she needed.

She was annoyingly proud and took great pleasure in her own self-reliance. Eventually, after having to cut short a private helicopter trip and picnic at the bottom of the Grand Canyon, because she had a shift at the restaurant, I bought the restaurant. Anonymously of course. I increased everyone's pay by non-life-changing amounts, hired more staff and tripled everyone's holiday entitlement. Problem solved.

We would spend more time in her apartment watching movies than we would spend at my house. She never felt comfortable with the sheer unnecessary scale of it and deemed it excessive in every way. I couldn't help but think what my ex, Nikki would have been doing with all this wealth.

'Pig in Shit' comes to mind. Don't get me wrong, most of us would be but it was just another reason I was falling so ridiculously in love with this woman.

And she did pay for our second meal together, despite me forgetting our deal and booking us a table at one of the most expensive bistros in Vegas. I insisted on paying the tip.

Time spent apart felt like wasted time. I would still go to the Basketball and the Golf club and the Casinos with friends when she was working or seeing her own friends, but it was always just killing time until I was picking her up or meeting her somewhere.

My year would be up in February. I had generously, and completely selfishly, paid for an extension to the shelter she was helping to build, and this would mean she would now be in Vegas longer than me.

Our Christmas together should have been perfect, and Jo had begrudgingly agreed to spend it with me at the house that I had decorated as a winter wonderland, complete with life-size, electronic Santa greeting guests in the hallway.

But it wasn't perfect. My deadline was looming. I wanted to throw up every time I thought about it. I would lay awake for hours, unable to push aside the feelings of loss I was already having.

She was of course revelling in our situation, oblivious of the guillotine of time hanging above us and simply enjoying that stage in a relationship when the other person is everything you need and not having air or food seemed more bearable. As time pushed on, the more she laughed the more I wanted to cry.

Come the 25th of December, we'd managed to find the Queen's Speech on one of the cable channels and drunkenly sung the national anthem whilst standing to attention in front of the giant TV. We stood there in thick, ridiculous woolly Christmas jumpers as the sixty-degree heat pressed against the windows outside. Collapsing backwards onto the sofa in a heap, I glanced at my watch to check when the Christmas pudding I was burning would be ready. As realisation dawned that the answer to my question was 'ten minutes ago', the watch ticked over another day:

'0 4 7'

As the eight became a seven it felt like someone had smashed a hammer into my chest.

Fortunately, as well as having slipped into a Turkey induced coma, Jo was tipsy enough not to notice me become quiet and withdrawn for the rest of Christmas day. I just couldn't shift the feeling though. I managed to pass off a subdued Boxing Day as being hungover and tired, but by the 27th, I knew I had to do something to drag myself from under the black cloud I was now permanently tethered to.

I called my contact at the airfield, chartered a Helicopter, and told Jo to be ready to leave in ten minutes.

My new Bugatti Veron had us at the Helicopter in less than eight minutes and within half an hour of making the call we were airborne and banking over the top of New York, New York, the Luxor and Camelot hotels as we headed West and over the desert towards L.A.

A day of extravagant spending on Rodeo Drive and its high-end boutique shops and eateries served to subdue the sense of impending doom, but it remained, nonetheless. I even found myself picking petty fights with Jo, predominantly over her refusal to let me lavish her with expensive purchases. I pondered on the flight back, as we detoured high above a section of the Colorado River, whether I was trying to cause problems between us and make the inevitable less painful when it came.

As was always the case, however, Jo brushed these off with her usual good humour, and I found it impossible to be anything but utterly in love with her.

Laden with bags and boxes, we arrived back at the house and made our way to the kitchen, which was part of the large open plan living section at the rear of the house. As Jo dropped her packages on the marble floor with an exhausted sigh, I clicked the kettle on. I didn't trust the 'hot water tap' that instantly provided boiling water, having written it off as Witchcraft on my first day in the house.

It was something about the way she looked at me as she put her hands on the small of her back as she straightened. Her hair had fallen across most of her face, and she attempted, in vain, to blow it away with the corner of her mouth. A habit I never tired of. She noticed me watching her and smiled the way she always did that left me incapable of anything other than being completely at her mercy. In that instant, she was the only thing that mattered.

The only thing.

"I need you to sit down for a sec," I said, failing miserably for it not to sound too ominous.

As you would expect, Jo's expression instantly changed to one of concern.

"What's up, honey?" she asked, pulling a stool from under a breakfast bar and hopping onto it.

"There's something I need to talk to you about, well, to tell you actually."

I looked down at my watch.

'0 4 5'

"I'm going away soon. For a while. Actually, I don't know how long. In forty-five days. It's all to do with where I get my money from."

As I finished my sentence, an ear-splitting crash came from the entrance hall, loud enough for us both to go rushing from the kitchen. In the middle of the hallway itself were a million shards of glass. The grand chandelier that ordinarily hung thirty feet above the hallway floor and dominated the entrance to the house, was laid, obliterated on the Persian rug below. A hole big enough for a man to climb through gaped in the ceiling above, and it had pulled the right arm off the giant Santa on its descent.

"How the hell does that happen?" Jo asked hands on her head in disbelief.

I had a pretty good idea. Consequences.

"Fuck your consequences," I said under my breath. The whole ten and a half months suddenly felt like a cruel trick and all rational thought deserted me.

"What did you say?" Jo said.

"Nothing. Look, don't worry about that for now, I'll get Maria to call someone tomorrow. What I need to tell you is really important."

"Yeah sure, but don't you think we need to do something with this, someone could really hurt themselves?" And she stooped to pick up a particularly nasty looking piece of glass

116

that was protruding above some others like a crystal blade. As Jo reached for it, she suddenly winced backwards and grasped one hand in the other. I instantly saw dark red blood seep between the gap in her fingers.

Consequences.

"Shit, I don't think I even touched it," she said, looking down at the vicious shard.

It was too much of a coincidence. That it was a warning was of no doubt. The power of the forces who held my very existence in their hands had been made blatantly and deliberately apparent to me. A drop of Jo's blood dripped and splashed onto the tiled floor.

"That'll scar," Jo said matter-of-factly, as we ran the half-inch gash on her right hand under a tap in the kitchen and watched the white porcelain gradually turn pink.

Jo sat back on her stool; hand wrapped in paper towels having instructed me to stop fussing.

"You said you have to go somewhere? Before the chandelier fell, something to do with work?"

I felt shaken by the smashed chandelier and the sight of Jo's blood.

The desire to tell Jo the truth drained from me.

"Yep, got the annual board meeting, just something I need to go to as the major shareholder. It's the only thing I need to do but it's quite important apparently. And it's coming up soon."

"Back in England?" Jo asked.

"Yeah, London. Hopefully won't be away too long. How's the hand looking?"

I owned everything it was possible to own, could do anything it was possible to do and yet had never felt so impotent, never less in control of my own destiny. I became distracted with thoughts of what would happen next. Potentially losing Jo forever in just a few weeks seemed inconceivable as we'd spent almost every day together for six months. I even asked myself if I would have been better off never meeting Diego in Churchill's, or even Jo in the restaurant that night.

I felt like I'd already lost enough, both my parents even Nikki. What had I done in a previous life to deserve this? Surely an appalling 'sick record' didn't justify this level of punishment. My situation was feeling more like a curse than a gift.

I kept telling myself I would come up with something, some plan for us to still be together once my watch clicked over to zero, or for me to remain in Las Vegas as Marcus Taylor forever.

I became more anxious when not spending time with Jo knowing that the time was potentially a priceless commodity. I flew us to the *real* Paris where we ate at the summit of the *real* Eiffel Tower before chartering a private boat for a sail along the Seine. I also managed to cram in skiing in Aspen, although being my first time it was predominantly falling over in Aspen, snorkelling in the Bahamas, and even a weekend in the secluded cove of a luxury resort in Hawaii.

I threw vast sums of money at the problem of trying to mask the reality of the impending and devastating situation. By the time we returned from Hawaii, that was just two days away.

I realised I had no idea how the transition was going to take place and perhaps never really considered it properly until those last couple of days. Where would I end up? What if I were with Jo at the time, could she come with me even? What would happen to the life I left here, to Marcus Taylor?

Too many questions.

I was sat in a deck chair in my garden, close to where the ice sculpture of Deonte had been on the first night that I saw the house, as my watch clicked over:

'0 0 1'

Jo was halfway through the breakfast shift at the restaurant, but every part of my being needed to see her. I didn't care about her irritating conscientiousness or who might have to cover her shift. We had agreed that I would pick her up after work, but this now felt a lifetime away.

I was going to get her.

The only question was whether or not I decided to tell her some version of the truth, something that would adequately explain why when she awoke tomorrow morning, there was a good chance I would be gone. Forever.

The first time Jo had told me she loved me was in the tiny lounge-diner of her apartment. I'd stayed over the previous evening, and she was curled up in my t-shirt watching cartoons. I'd leaned over the top of the sofa, kissed her on the head and handed her a steaming mug of tea. She took the tea and gazed up at me.

"I love you," she said, in such a relaxed and easy manner it caught me off guard.

"It's only a cup of tea. And it's not even got the Soya milk you like!" I said, surprised.

"No, I do. I have since that first breakfast, I think. I just wanted you to know. It's hard for me to say it after what happened, but I do."

Jo and I had spoken briefly about losing her husband, but the subject always changed before too much detail was discussed and old wounds opened. It was something I think we both deliberately avoided discussing. I know deep down she felt guilty for moving on.

"I know there's lots of stuff we need to talk through at some point but we've got plenty of time for that haven't we?"

I knelt behind Jo and reached my arms around, completely engulfing her. I didn't answer her. I'd never lied to her before and wasn't going to start now.

"I love you too," I said.

That had been three months ago.

I sprung from the chair and hurried back into the house for my phone and car keys. I'd just tell her and her manager that it was a family emergency. I had about fifteen minutes between now and then to work out what I would tell her after that. How had I left it so long before doing something about this? I suddenly felt like I hadn't been seeing things clearly for the last few weeks, existing in a daze almost. Perhaps that was no accident. Perhaps it was part of the transition.

I took the keys to a Mercedes, only because it was already parked out front having been valeted that morning and dashed back to the kitchen to pick up my phone that was charging on the sideboard.

Fourteen missed calls.

Seven texts.

Two voicemails.

All from Jo.

I listened to the first voicemail as I ran out of the front door and jumped in the Mercedes. The sound of Jo's voice moved from the handset by my ear to the Bluetooth in the car as the engine growled into life.

"Marcus, call me back when you can. It's urgent. It's my mum. Call me back please, I've sent you a few texts."

I sped down the drive as the second voicemail started.

"Hi, me again, I'm on my way to the airport," the voice crackled over the car speakers.

"Don't know if you've seen the texts yet but my dad called me earlier this morning. It's my mum, she's had an accident at work, a serious accident." Jo's voice broke, not the reception in the car but because she was struggling to hold back tears.

"They aren't sure she is going to make it. I've managed to get a flight to Heathrow that leaves at twenty past eleven. Please call me as soon as you can."

I looked at the electronic clock on the dashboard:

11:06

"Call Jo," I said to the car.

"*Do you want to call Jo?*" the polite electronic voice repeated back to me.

"YES!" I screamed back.

"*Calling Jo on 07…*"

By the time the car had repeated the number back to me, I was in a state of almost total panic.

The phone started ringing. I wasn't too late.

But there was only one ring before I heard her voice.

"Hi, this is Jo, I can't take your call, you know what to do."

11:07

Her plane was leaving in just thirteen minutes now. I irrationally found myself speeding towards the airport.

"Read texts," I commanded the car hurriedly.

The first few were requests for me to call Jo as soon as possible. The next couple explained that she had tried to call me as something had happened at home in England.

The polite electronic voice finally read text seven of seven:

"Need to turn the phone off now plane taking off in a mo will call when I land love you ex ex ex."

11:09

I pulled over into a lay-by by the side of the road about a mile from the airport. I was never going to make it.

I wondered briefly who I could call and pay ten million dollars to ground that plane.

I was googling flight times from Las Vegas to Heathrow ten minutes later when I saw a Virgin Atlantic plane climbing towards the clouds above the Strip. Jo was on that plane. I knew she was.

What followed was the longest ten hours of my life. Ten hours before the flight landed in the UK. Ten agonising hours of waiting for Jo to call. I paced the house for most of it. Not the last day as Marcus Taylor I had planned.

I sent all the staff home and walked the marble floors drinking straight from a bottle of red wine. I had no idea how or when my time as Marcus would end. I just hoped and prayed it wouldn't be until after I had spoken to her.

Eventually, after forever, the time came when Jo's flight was due to land. I managed to control myself and leave it another three and a half minutes before calling her.

Voicemail.

Hadn't turned the phone on yet.

The plane still taxiing.

I decided in that instance that I would tell her everything come what may. What could be worse than simply disappearing and her never knowing? My stomach churned as I called Jo's number again and again with the same result.

"Hi, this is Jo, I can't take your call, you know what to do."

I felt completely powerless. I didn't even know what hospital Jo's mum would be at to try and reach her there, all I knew was that her parents lived in West London somewhere.

Five minutes, then ten minutes, then fifteen minutes past.

Still no answer from Jo. Still, no call from Jo.

I quickly found a website with flight information and searched for Virgin flights to Heathrow that had left that morning. There it was. *'Virgin Atlantic Flight 867. Delayed landing. Holding pattern.'*

There was simply no way this was all just coincidence. The accident, the timing, missing the calls, the landing delay. All on what was my last day? All having had decided to tell Jo everything regardless of the consequences?

I felt powerless because I was powerless. The forces working against me were irresistible.

The knowledge that I wasn't going to be able to speak to Jo when it came, came with a strangely calm acceptance.

I was therefore surprised when my phone buzzed in my hand an hour later. But not surprised when I read the message from a number I didn't recognise.

"Hi it's me, battery died, just got through passport control. Borrowed a nice lady's phone to text you, gonna jump in a cab. Will try and find a charger at the hospital."

I knew then for certain that I would never see or speak to Jo again.

Stood on the lawn of the house, the sun has dropped below the jagged horizon, the only sound was the faint whirring of the swimming pool pump. From my position, I could see almost all of the hotels on the Las Vegas Strip and the 'Stratosphere' pointing skyward towards the eastern end. The lights from Caesars Palace and The Bellagio were illuminating the twilight.

I could see the pinnacle of the Paris hotel and the pyramidion of the Luxor. I checked my phone again. Nothing from Jo as expected, but a text from one of the fixers at the Venetian asking if I wanted to get involved in a game of Texas Hold 'em tomorrow evening with some Chinese businessman. Another message was a text from the Basketball club asking if I was planning on using my box for the game this weekend.

The heat was oppressive, and I peeled off my shirt before sitting down on the cool grass. It was damp from where the sprinklers had been doing their thing since sunset.

I suddenly felt exhausted. Tiredness I'd never experienced swept over me and my eyes felt like someone had tied weights to them. I thought it would be OK if I lay down. Just for a minute. I balled my shirt up and rested my head on it. I could feel the wet grass seeping into my shorts. It would be fine. I'd just be a minute. Perhaps I could even shut my eyes. Just for a minute. I'd try Jo again once this feeling passed.

Chapter 11

The first difference I noticed was my hair.

On waking, Marcus Taylor's mop of ordinarily perfect hair, would be tousled and knotted and likely covering one or both eyes. Therefore, I'd formed a habit, on waking, of sweeping it up and out of the way.

As I became aware of my consciousness, however, I pushed the hair away that wasn't there. My first and completely irrational thought was that some friends had come to the house, found me on the lawn and shaved my head.

I'd dreamt that Jo and I were in her apartment watching something on TV. Except for her apartment in the dream was the bedroom I'd had as a boy, and Jo didn't look like Jo, but my old English teacher Mr Jameson. I tried to push the mental image from my mind.

I left the room for some reason but when I returned it was a different room and Jo/Mr Jameson was gone. The image on the TV screen was of my mum. The depth of sadness that overwhelmed me as I entered the new room woke me instantly.

I didn't move initially. I could already feel a heavy duvet pressing down on me and my head sunk into lush, plump pillows before I opened my eyes. As I did so, I saw walls hung with red drapes, and ornate pillars supporting a ceiling decorated with intricate paintings of what looked like Bedouin camps, palm trees and desert-dwelling animals. A picture of a white and gold Arab stallion stood majestically on its hind legs, filled the far wall.

I allowed myself a moment to let the feeling of disorientation pass before removing a hand from under the duvet. It was huge. Long, thick fingers and a palm the size of a saucer. I sat up.

The rest of the room was much the same as the slither I had seen from the pillow.

More pillars stretched away to a staircase leading up to what seemed to be a second floor. Gold leaf decorated every piece of furniture, and I could see three separate seating areas, all slightly different shades of red and finished with mountains of cushions and throws. The small amount of light from the room was coming from a shard of sunlight piercing two drawn curtains to my left, across a floor covered with an enormous red and gold rug.

Sat up, I could see down my torso. Bulging pecs and a six-pack you could drive a car over. My arms were like veiny slabs of meat and as I flexed my biceps, I couldn't prevent a smile.

I took another moment to gather myself. I could be anywhere. Nervous apprehension was wrestling with a feeling of loss and my mind began to race with thoughts of what to do about Jo. There were dozens of courses of action I could take, but I suspected my intentions would be known before I knew them myself and all doors closed to me.

I suspected I would have to bide my time. I squeezed my eyes shut and fought the urge to scream Jo's name. I had been 'reborn' and felt every bit the helpless child.

I stepped onto the cold tiled floor and grabbed a robe that was draped across the foot of the bed. The arms stretched only just past my elbow and the length left little to the imagination. I guessed I must have been around 6'5" and 250 lb of predominantly muscle. It would take some getting used to, but I have to admit I liked the idea of being the biggest guy in the room. For a year anyway.

Despite the confusing cocktail of emotions, I was apprehensively excited about where I might be and what I might see when I pulled the curtains back. It wasn't lost on me what I must have looked like as I tiptoed across that room, a giant of a man in a tiny robe, trying to make as little contact with his size 14 feet on the cold floor as possible.

I pulled open a slightly larger gap where the curtains met, and the brightness forced me to turn away and shield my eyes. I thought I'd burned my retinas out and was going to spend a year as the Planet's richest blind man.

Sweeping both curtains aside now, it took me only a few seconds to work out where I was.

I was approximately fifty floors up. To my left and my right, the perfect blue waters of the Indian Ocean rippled gently and lapped against the sandy beaches far below me. The water was not only on either side but behind me also. The manmade island I was on was joined to the beach by a narrow bridge about a hundred metres long.

A flat desert landscape stretched infinitely into the distance, but the immediate view was of ostentatious hotel complexes, marinas packed with superyachts and villas, all uniquely designed and increasingly vast.

A few years back, Nikki and I had stood on the beach below where I was now and looked up at this place with its helipad, tennis court roof and six-star accommodation.

I was in the Burj Al Arab Hotel, 'The Sail' as it was known, and the view from my suite was of Dubai and the Arabian desert beyond.

I stood in front of a full-length mirror. Short mousey blonde hair, almost a buzz cut, a full beard of the same colour and a ruggedly handsome face. As much as I was feeling indescribable anger towards whoever or whatever was controlling my life now and snatched Jo away from me, they, or 'It', had come up trumps with the physical package again.

Much as with my first transition, I made my way to some colossal wardrobes that stood imposingly against another wall. Clothes bulged from all three and contained everything the discerning traveller could need. I dressed in a t-shirt Marcus Taylor could have used as a tent and some smart looking shorts. Looking back over my shoulder and out of the window, I also grabbed some sunglasses and perched them on my head.

On the bedside table was a wallet. Sat on top of the wallet was the watch.

'3 6 5'

I grabbed them both and made my way up the staircase to the second floor which was another seating area with a bar and a bathroom the size of my old apartment.

A muzak version of Sonny and Cher's *'I've got you babe'* was playing through some speakers built into the wall.

I sat myself on the edge of a roll-top bath that even with my new stature, looked big enough for me to drown in if I happened to doze off while enjoying a soak.

Flipping open the leather wallet, it was much the same as my first time around. A driver's licence and a credit card.

The name on both read:

'Mark Vickers'

The date of birth was the same as my own and Marcus's had been.

I slapped the wallet closed and slid it into the pocket of my shorts.

Composing myself, I stood tall and managed, with relative success, to squash the feeling of loss and confusion away in a little box in my mind. Just for now, I told myself, *'just for now'*.

A few minutes later, a loud rapping on the bedroom door pulled me away from the view of Dubai that I was taking in whilst trying to decide what to do next.

I knew who that would be.

Juan.

Come to remind me of his 'Laws' and drop some pearls of wisdom before deserting me to try and muddle through another year on my own.

Quite frankly, he could fuck off.

"Go away, please!" I shouted in a deep but sing-songy voice. "I'm not interested! Thank you!"

The door knocked again, no louder or more aggressively, just exactly the same as the first time.

"I've told you, go away please, I don't need your bullshit, you have ruined my life, thank you," I said, continuing in the melodic, up and down, 'I'm not listening' tone.

Silence for something like ten seconds.

Then another knock, perhaps a little slower and more tentative this time.

As I stomped over to the door, I wondered if 'Beings' that could control space and time could also take a well-placed right hook.

"You've got a fucking cheek!" I shouted, opening the door hard enough to almost pull it off its hinges.

"My apologies Sir, I was asked to deliver this to you."

A small and slight dark-skinned chap in hotel uniform was stood with one hand behind his back and the other balancing an ice bucket containing a bottle of Dom Perignon.

"Oh, god, I'm really sorry mate, chuck it down there. I thought you were someone else," I said sheepishly.

He placed the bucket on a coffee table and set to leave.

"Hang on. One sec."

I reached my hand into my pocket and pulled out the wallet. Where there had been no cash before, there was now a wad of notes.

"Here," I said, pulling one of them out and handing it to the man. One hundred Dirhams. I couldn't recall the Sterling to AED exchange rate, my previous trip had been some time ago, but I hoped it wasn't a life-changing amount. I passed the note slowly looking for a reaction from the man.

He looked genuinely pleased but didn't break down or try and hug me, so I took that as a good sign that I hadn't just given him enough money to buy a house on the beach. Note to self: *'Check the exchange rates before doing anything else'*.

He bowed his head before leaving and pulled the door closed behind him.

There was a note taped to the bucket:

Hi Mark, hope you like your new name, sorry I didn't meet you first thing but I didn't feel like getting punched in the face! ;)

Remember what I said, everyone gets what they deserve one way or the other!

Your carriage awaits, get in the lift and press 'UP'.

Your friend, Juan.

'Everyone gets what they deserve' I read again but still failed to see what I'd done to deserve feeling this amount of despair. The cruelness of being made to feel like this in a situation that should have been anything but, just made it incomprehensibly worse. I doubted very much that Jo or her poor Mother had done anything bad enough to warrant what they had been put through over the last twenty-four hours for the purpose of teaching me a lesson. I desperately hoped they were both OK although Jo had sounded as if there was an inevitability to her mum's situation.

I resigned myself to being a pawn in whoever's game this was a little longer and made my way out of the room.

After a brief journey skywards, the lift doors opened onto an open area of the roof of the hotel. The cloudless blue sky looked too perfect to be real, painted almost. A couple were playing tennis on the court off to my left that was set into a large disc, barely bigger in diameter than a standard tennis court and actually protruded from the hotel itself, floating high above the Indian Ocean.

As I watched, a particularly fast serve from one of the players flew past the opponent and, after bouncing once, disappeared over the side of the disc with nothing to stop it but the water fifty floors below. Despite the unfathomable wealth of the hotel's owners and many of its guests, it was still hard not to find the amount of tennis balls that must be lost, terribly wasteful.

The temperature was such that I could feel my own skin cooking on my bones, and I ducked my head and made my way across the roof to my 'carriage' which was a black and yellow chopper, blades already spinning noisily and invisibly in the centre of a giant 'H'.

I climbed up in a seat behind the pilot who was sitting stoically staring ahead in huge aviator sunglasses and a helicopter headset.

Without checking to see if I was all set and buckled up, the helicopter began to lift off. I fumbled for straps and clasps, swore a bit, tried to force a clip into the wrong hole, swore a bit more and eventually managed to join two bits together that seemed to fit. The Chopper dipped left and wallowed right before rising into the sky and above the hotel's 'mast'.

Once at its required height, it banked hard and right and looped all the way around the hotel before dipping its nose and heading along the coast. I'd ridden in helicopters a good few times over the last twelve months but the way the pilot was chucking this little bird around was making me want to redecorate the inside with the contents of my stomach.

I could see the man-made 'Palm' Island draw closer with its luxury houses and Atlantis hotel at its apex. Thankfully and within no time at all, we began to slow. The chopper moved into a hover above a helipad at the end of a jetty. This jetty was at the Southern end of a Marina that was rammed full of yachts of all sizes.

I say all sizes, however, what I mean is from bloody massive to the size of a small town. The largest of them all had five floors that I could see above sea level and looked to be at least five hundred feet long.

As we began to descend, I could see a swimming pool, jacuzzi and dance floor on one of its decks and a number of crew in pressed white uniforms milling around, busy at their work.

"Big innit, Boss?" the pilot said, turning in his seat and pointing a thumb at the superyacht.

"You!" I shouted into the microphone on my headset.

Juan grinned inanely and pulled his sunglasses off his face.

"Certainly is, Boss! Long-time no see!"

"You bastard!" I bellowed and lunged forward, grabbing the back of his neck with my baseball mitt sized hand. The desperate feelings of the day before, the 'accident' to Jo's mum, the whole thing became too much in that instant, and I shook his head like a rag doll. The chopper, now around fifteen feet from the helipad, dipped violently left and right, backwards and forwards.

"Wooah there big guy!" Juan managed to croak out, red-faced, veins popping from his neck and face. "You'll kill us both!"

I couldn't tell if he was laughing or crying but as he said that, the right-hand landing gear bounced off the tarmac and threw me backwards into my seat. I sat there, apoplectic, breathing heavily and every bit as red-faced as Juan who was fighting to level the chopper and set it down on the helipad.

As it settled on solid ground, blades revolving, Juan leaned forward out of my reach and turned to face me again. His usual irritatingly boyish manner and expression were replaced with something else more akin to sympathy.

"You are shooting the messenger here my friend," he continued morosely. "I'm only ever here to try and help you. You aren't my only boss, Mike."

As he said that, he glanced skyward before looking back at me. "I wish I could tell you more but if I go 'off-script', I'm toast. Literally."

There was a softness and genuineness to the way he spoke that took the edge from my anger and made me want to launch him into the sea slightly less. He nodded to my door as he took off his headset and set it down in the passenger seat. I did the same, swung the door open and jumped out of the helicopter as the blades began to slow.

Stooping, we both made our way towards the entrance to the Jetty, standing straight only once clear of the helipad. I noticed that Juan was keeping himself out of swinging distance, however.

135

"I'm not the bad guy here Mike," Juan began, rubbing his neck. "I don't make the rules, but you did know them when you got into this thing."

"I didn't sign up for you people, or whatever the fuck you are, to hurt the people I love!"

I took a step forward, fists balled, and Juan took a mirroring step backwards. "How was hurting Jo's mother part of the bargain?" I demanded.

"She's fine. She got a nasty bang on the head that will turn out to be nowhere near as serious as first thought. In fact, while in hospital, a Doctor will notice a lump that would have become life-threatening if it hadn't been spotted this soon and give her another twenty years."

I didn't know what to believe and had no way of finding out if what he was saying was true or not. I knew that whatever I did would be because that's what they wanted me to do, I'd see what they wanted me to see.

"You were going to tell her Mike. They knew you were before you did."

Perhaps I was. I'd never now been certain.

With little choice in the matter and the added bonus of it making me feel less guilty, I convinced myself that he was telling the truth about Jo's mum.

The sun was beating down on us both and sweat was forming on all parts of my huge frame.

"Perhaps we should get inside," I said.

Juan looked at me apprehensively, gauging whether or not he was safe from further attack.

"Ahhh!" Juan said. "Now there's a good idea."

I followed him along the jetty to a junction. Straight ahead was a complex that housed the harbour master, restaurants, bars, and shops and taking a right would lead to a row of moored yachts, including the monster with the five decks.

Without pausing a beat, Juan turned right.

"I really do need to get out of this heat Juan, I'll be back to Mike Barnes size if I'm out here much longer," I said, wiping sweat from my brow on the stretched sleeve of my T-shirt.

Juan ignored me, and I continued to follow dutifully behind until we reached the merciful shade of the Super Yacht.

"What do you think?" Juan said, facing the giant boat, arms outstretched.

From this close, I couldn't even see both ends and only the first two decks.

"I dunno, it's really big I suppose?"

"*It's really big I suppose?*" Juan said, mimicking me "It's not just '*really big*' it's the biggest bloody yacht in the world!" Juan put his hands on his hips and shook his head.

The biggest in the world? I thought, now trying to take in its enormity. I wondered who owned it? A Sheikh, Russian Oligarch, Tech Billionaire?

"It's yours," Juan said as if reading my mind. "Your lack of imagination in Vegas made me feel so sad I couldn't watch you waste another year. Out of interest, how many times *did* you leave Nevada in the twelve months?"

I knew the answer to that. It was six. Six times in twelve months. I'd meant to be more adventurous but when you have everything you need at your fingertips it's easy for plans to get pushed back. And back. And back....

I ignored his question.

"When you say *mine*?"

"Yours," Juan replied. "Something to get you started, somewhere to live until you get somewhere else. Something to take your mind off the past and see the possibilities of the future. This thing will take you anywhere you want to go in the world. For Pete's sake, use it."

Juan motioned for me to follow him further along the jetty and around the back of the boat. At the bottom of the steps leading up to the first deck, a short woman was stood in what I recognised as naval uniform. White trousers, white short-sleeved shirt complete with epaulettes and wide-brimmed flat hat with anchor insignia above the peak.

Under normal circumstances a woman dressed in a tight uniform and smiling at me would have caused an instinctive 'stirring' and flirting would have been an automatic physical response but I was in some sort of mourning for Jo and the moment passed.

"Good Morning Mr Vickers," the woman said in an unmistakable Aussie accent, from behind her shades.

"Welcome aboard, I'm Captain Antoinette Deeney. But you can call me Toni." Stood in front of me, she barely reached my ribcage but there was a presence and confidence in her that instantly made you feel reassured. I thought about what sort of person could skipper a vessel of this size. I couldn't even parallel park my Fiat Uno.

We all three stepped aboard and climbed the long shallow steps up to the first deck where the crew, what looked to be about sixty or so people, had formed into a guard of honour on either side of the walkway.

Feeling extremely self-conscious, I nodded and mumbled thanks as I moved between the lines.

On being dismissed by their Captain, the crew dispersed in all directions and were quickly back to their jobs.

Captain Deeney spent the next hour giving me a tour of my new home while Juan followed along behind, occasionally pointing things out with a smug expression, clearly pleased with himself and his purchase.

We arrived on a deck that had been prepared for a meal for Juan and I, and the Captain left us, disappearing into the cavernous boat.

As I sat, I noticed the Burj Khalifa, the world's tallest building, in the Dubai haze beyond the Marina. In a city of extraordinarily tall structures, the Khalifa seemed to pierce the clouds themselves.

"We need to talk," Juan said, tearing into a baguette and avoiding looking me in the eye. "You're feeling an unnatural range of emotions and having too many conflicting thoughts at the moment. This is your third persona in 366 days and it's a lot to take in."

Of course, he was right. I'd now been Mike, Marcus and Mark. I was struggling to detach myself from thoughts of Jo and my mind raced with what she might be thinking and possible ways to contact her. I reached out for a glass to pour some water and knocked the glass across the table and into a bowl of olives. Using arms the length of legs was going to take some getting used to.

It was almost impossible to accept where I was and what I was doing as real. Could I just sail back to Vegas or even London, to find Jo and tell her everything? Could I call Jo right now? I knew the answer to both those things was 'no'. Every permutation of contacting Jo would somehow lead to consequences, not just for me but potentially for her, as I'd already seen. Did I really just have to let her go?

I couldn't face the food, a feeling of nausea and the heat, even under the canopy stretched out above us, made eating almost impossible.

"It will take you a few days, maybe not even that, and you'll be fine. Just relax, get used to being Mark Vickers and embrace it all."

Easier said than done, I thought.

Juan continued "The first one is always the toughest. You throw yourself into your new life, make attachments and even put down roots. You'll learn not to do that. Don't blow this by being all… all… human."

"So, what now then?" I asked.

"Whatever you want. I suggest we see what Dubai has to offer to the discerning trillionaire and take it from there?"

I picked up a breadstick and managed to nibble at the end without throwing up. I took that as a good sign.

"So, Diego just did this for almost forty years?"

"It gets easier, and you quickly get accustomed to life the money allows. It becomes as necessary as oxygen. Answer me this Mike, after just one year, can you even imagine having to work eight hours a day, just to put a roof over your head and food on your table?" With that, he grabbed a chicken leg and ripped a chunk from it like a medieval King.

I couldn't of course. For the last year of my life, nothing had been impossible. If I didn't have something, I bought it. Even friends. If I couldn't do something, I paid someone to do it for me. As much as not having Jo with me felt like someone had ripped my heart out, I also couldn't imagine going back to my old life cleaning pools as Mike Barnes. In fact, the very thought terrified me.

I knew that I had to have a different mindset if this was going to prove to be more of a blessing than a curse but it was easier said than done. I felt ashamed of myself for having any sort of negative emotions when most people would give anything to have had what I had. Despite that, I still had to force back thoughts of Jo. I consoled myself with the fact that when the time came, I could simply do what Diego did and pass the 'gift' to someone else.

However, I couldn't even imagine doing that as I sat on the deck of that boat, a feast laid out before me and the Indian Ocean behind, an infinite sea of potential and possibilities.

My chest physically ached with how much I already missed Jo, but the futility of holding those feelings wasn't lost on me. The conflicting emotions and perspectives threatened to tear me in half.

"What about Marcus Taylor?" I asked. "What about the life he had? People relied on him, somebody loved him," I managed to suppress what could easily have become tears.

Juan considered this for a moment before answering.

"It's difficult to describe in a way you'd understand. When someone leaves an incarnation, it creates issues, as you say. Let's call them 'wrinkles. These 'wrinkles' just get *ironed* out. A text or email here, a memory altered there. Nothing to unbalance the natural order of things too much. But just enough for things to carry on without you."

A sickening thought suddenly hit me.

"Will she remember me?"

"Of course. But she will likely be kept distracted for a while, have other things on her mind. One or two memories of you tweaked. All just enough that she doesn't spend too much time looking for you and create more wrinkles."

Juan looked at me for perhaps four or five seconds before continuing, "She *will* be fine."

I looked back at Juan and believed him. If they could do all this, then manipulating Jo's perspective on a few things was a walk in the park I imagine. What was clear was that we were all just puppets in somebody's cosmic Punch and Judy show. At that point, I felt like it was just my turn to play Punch.

Did I want her to miss me as I missed her? I wanted her to be happy but the thought of her not feeling the same way about me anymore crushed me. Worse still, what about when she eventually found someone else.

I selfishly decided I did want her to miss me. A lot.

I couldn't see that there was any possibility that this was all coming from a place of good, a place of compassion. The hurt, the manipulations, the 'consequences'. Until this point in my life, I'd had no time for unseen powers or the forces of 'good' and 'evil', but I was in no doubt that my situation was being designed and dictated from a place where the latter presided.

Chapter 12

I learned to keep my distance from people. Not only did it prevent potential complications at the end of Mark Vickers journey, but it made tripping over an ill-conceived back story less likely. When asked where I had accumulated my wealth, I would simply answer that it was inherited from a family that had invested shrewdly in some of the household name tech firms, before moving the conversation on. It was amazing how a subtle facial expression could stop further interrogation, particularly when people were keen not to upset 6'5" Trillionaire Mark Vickers.

Despite my hardening exterior, it proved impossible not to think of Jo and what she might be doing. Whom she might be doing it with.

Dubai, despite some similarities, felt a world away from Las Vegas. The heat was similar, that raw, oppressive, desert heat and the same luxury cars would blast up and down the Sheikh Zayed Road as they did the Las Vegas Boulevard, but the differences were fundamental. For a start, gambling was illegal and there were certainly no overt sexual overtones, to what was fundamentally a Muslim country, where it had been the very heartbeat of Vegas.

Both things were available if you knew where to look, however. Within a couple of weeks of being there and dining at certain clubs and restaurants owned by certain locals, I found myself sat at poker tables and blackjack tables surrounded by beautiful women of all nationalities, often in various states of undress and very much for the patrons to use for their own pleasure. However weird and wonderful that might be. These places were usually accessed via heavily guarded doors and very much by invitation only.

On the streets outside, it was illegal to hold hands.

Juan had stayed on the boat for the first 48 hours before leaving me to my own devices again. At breakfast on day three, rather than Juan being sat there in his helicopter pilot's uniform, one of the crew brought me a note from him on a silver platter. In the note, he implored me to make the most of my time as Mark Vickers and wished me luck.

I was on my own again. As frustrating as he could be, I felt sad that he had gone. I decided my autobiography would be called 'The Lonely Trillionaire' as I tore into a Croissant, feeling sorry for myself on my $1 bn Super Yacht.

I spent the next few days starting conversations with other yacht owners in the Marina bar or stopping for a chat with people as they lounged or worked on their own boats. This was how I received the invites, first to the bars and restaurants but later to the underground clubs. More often than not, they were frequented by local Politicians and high-ranking Police officers as well as most of the world's 'Rich List'. The Dubai of the Water Parks, indoor Ski Slopes, Shopping Malls and 'Desert 4x4 Safari's' was very much just one side of the coin.

I began to hear stories of far-flung and exotic places visited by other yacht owners as well as forcing Toni, my boat's captain, to regale me with tales of some of the places she had seen in her years on the Oceans. Although at times it was as much for the company as genuine interest. I'll admit to looking at the Ship's Captain in a not always professional capacity but she subtly managed to purvey a 'hands off' demeanour without being rude or stand-offish.

Years of practice I imagine. She would speak passionately of South America, the Far East, Africa and her home, the East Coast of Australia. After a month of living a life not too dissimilar to the one that I'd lead in Las Vegas, I decided to raise anchor and see the world.

As the giant boat eased away from the Dubai Marina, I stood at the very front, or bow, as Toni pointed out to me with slight exasperation later that evening.

"I'm the King of the world!" I couldn't help myself shouting as the back swung out, and I was facing Dubai for the last time. Thinking I had been alone, I turned to see a crew member cleaning the deck behind me who looked only marginally less embarrassed than I did.

I got to know Captain Toni extremely well during our travels and it turned out she was a Wife and Mother as well as Sea Captain. She explained through watery eyes one evening, that she missed them all terribly but the 'gig just pays too well' and their plans were for her to do another two years before returning home and settling for a good with the hard-earned money. Her husband would send her photographs of their four-year-old daughter at least once every day, and they counted down the weeks until her current contract ended.

I asked if she would miss the open Seas, the adventures, the money? "Not as much as I miss my daughter." She replied, before finding something important to attend to that allowed her to park the conversation.

We headed East across the Arabian Sea towards the Indian Ocean, stopping first off the South Coast of Sri Lanka. Much of what I saw was a paradise. Miles of sandy white beaches lined with Palm trees and bursting with vibrant fauna of all colours.

I hopped between islands, at first on the speedboat which came with the Yacht but later the smaller motorboats owned by locals. They were grateful to try their English out on me, and I was grateful to be shown some of the beaches and coves normally inaccessible to tourists. Of course, I had to be careful not to tip life-changing amounts of money which were tricky when the average weekly wage was less than a pair of my pants.

I hired a guide, Roshan, or 'Rosh' as he told me to call him, a jolly little local fella with fewer teeth than fingers, and we headed inland for a few days, following the well-beaten tourist paths of temples and elephant rides. Sat on a rock or bench outside one of the many hilltop Buddhist temples we saw, it was impossible not to reflect on the comparison of my various lives and, of course when I wasn't able to prevent them, thoughts of Jo. The time spent with her had been the happiest of my life.

Whether that had been dining at the 'Stratosphere' restaurant or watching 'Friends' repeats in her apartment. I even spent some time thinking about Nikki and how we'd reached the point that we had. We'd been besotted with each other for the first few years and our plans took us all the way to the graveyard we'd be buried next to each other in for eternity.

But we were going through the motions long before she started cheating on me with the next-door neighbour. I was still angry for her betrayal, but the relationship had been as dead as a Dodo for years.

Despite this, I still hoped to be able to action some clever and scarring revenge on her at some point. I'd spent too many sleepless nights conjuring up all sorts of ways to even the score. No amount of walking around Buddhist temples was going to make me so chilled I didn't want her to feel the same pain she'd caused me.

Stood at the bottom of a particularly intimidating set of steps that lead up another hill to another temple, my guide, and I had a brief disagreement about the virtues of the climb. What became clear was that he wouldn't take no for an answer and so I eventually lost the argument to the man half my size.

I trudged wearily upwards for almost twenty minutes. The last hundred yards of winding steps was under a balcony of foliage, some under which I had to stoop. However, on emerging from the shade of the trees and now at the summit of the hill, I turned to see the landscape below. I immediately apologised to Rosh.

He had been absolutely right. An artist couldn't have painted a more perfect scene. Groves of fruit trees pressed up against meandering rivers that swept towards a crystal blue lake surrounded by the tiny houses of a village.

Mountains dominated the right-hand side of nature's canvass and these were blanketed with deep green pine trees and punctuated with rock formations billions of years old. I felt like I could have stood there on that hill for the rest of my life still not having taken in every detail.

Rosh walked me around the grounds of what was a working monastery of Buddhist monks. The simplicity of their lives was apparent but no more than their contentedness. I wondered what their secret was.

As we were about to descend, I spotted a much older monk in traditional orange robes, sitting cross-legged on a tattered mat, weaving some sort of basket. An identical one was sat on the ground in front of him, and I could see a few rupees laid in the bottom. Taking this to be a subtle request for a donation, I reached into my wallet and took out what I hoped was an appropriate amount of notes, before dropping them into the basket.

I did what all English people do at that point and made a strange shape with my face that I hoped said "There you go, sorry it's not more," but at the same time saying, "I am not doing this because I think I'm better than you or out of pity."

Not easy, but something we have been practising for thousands of years and passed down from generation to generation. Americans would chuck the notes in with a confident "There you go, pal!" We can only dream of such things.

"Thank you very much," the monk said in accented but near-perfect English as I turned to walk away.

"You're welcome," I replied, a little taken aback. "You are very lucky, you live in a very beautiful place," I continued in slow, clipped English, failing to not sound condescending.

"Yes, I am. Very lucky. I have everything here I need. And nothing more."

I thought about what he said for a moment. *'And nothing more'.*

"Would you mind passing me those?" He asked, gesturing to a small pile of leaves close to where I was standing.

I reached down, picked them up, and held them out to him. For a brief moment in time, we were both holding the leaves. At this moment, I shuddered, but not in the way you do when you are cold or scared but in a way that made me feel calm and at ease, the ache in my legs from the hike up the hill, gone, an almost subconscious concern I'd had about making it back to the Yacht before dark, gone, thoughts of loss, of revenge, gone.

As I let go of the leaves, however, the monk was looking at me with an expression of concern.

"You are on a journey," he said. "You are not the first man that I have met on this journey."

"That's right, I've come from the UAE, and after this, we are heading to Thailand and Vietnam and then maybe Australia?" I chose to assume I'd imagined the gravity he'd said it with.

"For some, the journey is short, but for others, it never ends," he continued, drawing a circle in the dirt with his finger as he spoke. He looked me in the eyes for what felt like an eternity.

It was more than philosophical mumbo jumbo. He *knew.* I felt he did.

A breeze rolled up the hillside as I stood in front of the old man, cross-legged on the floor.

"You will have a choice," he said. "I will pray that you make the right one."

My mind raced with questions. How did he know? Did that put me in trouble? Could he tell me any more than the vague information about my 'Journey' than Juan gave me?

As I tried to organise my thoughts, I heard Rosh speaking to someone nearby.

"Mr Mark!" he shouted, emerging from the side of a small building behind me.

As I turned and saw Rosh, a younger monk appeared next to the old man and helped him to his feet. The younger man looked into the basket. "Thank you," he said smiling. "But he must rest now, he is almost one hundred years old you know?"

"Wait!" I called after them as they shuffled off. "Will I be OK? That's all I want to know!"

The old monk turned cautiously and spoke.

"That depends on your choice."

He walked away, the younger monk supporting him with both arms, his love for the old man obvious for anyone to see.

Having said an emotional farewell to Rosh, we sailed from Sri Lanka and continued East towards Thailand, Toni having to make several phone calls, and unofficial payments to be able to moor in the ocean outside the Royal Phuket Marina. There weren't many places my yacht could actually drop anchor, such as its size. In some places, it would block access in and out of a Marina or harbour entirely. We had moored in one location close to the shore and managed to entirely block out the sun to a tiny fishing village.

I kept mulling over what the old man had said to me. I just hoped the importance of 'the choice' he mentioned when it came, was obvious and my entire future didn't depend on whether I turned left or right at a 'Stop' sign or whether or not I had Frosties or Rice Krispies for breakfast one day, the very existence of the Universe hanging on Tony the Tiger or those three little smiley twats.

My time in Sri Lanka had been a bit of a spiritual awakening. It was impossible not to be affected by the ambience of the places I had seen, the calmness of the monasteries, even the jovial and positive nature of Rosh, whom, despite not having the proverbial 'pot to piss in', was probably the happiest human I'd ever met. I considered this as I whipped across the surf in the yacht's speedboat, bouncing over the waves towards the shore where I was to be greeted with champagne and a chauffeur.

Whereas in Sri Lanka I had stayed on the boat and travelled from there every day, I decided to base myself on land in Thailand. This was also a good excuse to give the hard-working crew of the yacht, a few days 'R & R'.

Toni argued as I knew she would, but I insisted and threatened to fire her if she didn't spend some time away from 'the bloody boat' that she seemed to treat as a second child at times. I paid for everyone to stay at a five-star hotel in Phuket and chucked in a little 'play' money too.

I found Phuket a more challenging place to focus on my Chakras, such were the other temptations on offer. My payments, or to call them what they were 'bribes' for being able to moor up there, afforded me the company of some of the local dignitaries who had benefited from my arrival, and they took great pleasure in showing me *all* that Phuket had to offer.

I was introduced to one very talented young lady who was able to make me a Pina Colada without using her hands.

And I don't mean she had dextrous feet. I ordered a beer in the next round.

One afternoon, back in Vegas, Jo and I had ordered Pizza and watched the 'Beach' the Leonardo Di Caprio film where he discovers the most perfect beach in the world, here in Thailand. We half-joked about visiting the same place and trying to make the long swim across from the mainland that he and his travel companions do.

I discovered pretty quickly when enquiring about where the film was shot, that the beach itself didn't exist and was created by the magic of CGI. Disappointed, I nonetheless booked an internal flight to the part of Thailand where they'd made most of the film.

I travelled light and dressed down in some plain shorts and scruffy looking T-shirt, despite it having cost roughly the same as the flight had, from a trendy boutique in Dubai.

When I landed, I picked up the keys to a bright yellow convertible Lamborghini I'd arranged before I set off. Mark Vickers stature was such that I had to fold me into it and nearly dislocated a kneecap as I slammed the door closed.

I drove up and down the coastal road; I'd been directed to and managed to convince myself I recognised some of it from the movie. I stopped to hydrate a couple of times at roadside stalls and cafes, drawing a crowd of local kids on each occasion. I made the mistake of letting one of them sit in the driver's seat on one of the breaks and wasn't able to leave for another hour and once every other kid in the village, and a few adults, had their turn.

As the sun lowered in the sky and the heat became less angry, I was driving along the same coast road with the wind pleasantly buffeting my hair and face when I felt the first grumblings of hunger and decided to stop for a bite to eat. I saw a place that sat between the beach and the road and had a small dust car park. There were other people eating there, which I took as a good sign, and pulled over.

I took a plastic seat at a faded table on the sand and grabbed a menu. The usual tourist fayre was listed before me.

"Just a coke and a cheese and tomato toastie please mate," I said, as the waiter, who looked to be about ten years old, approached with pad and pen in hand.

"You got it, Mister!" He said, before bouncing back towards the café which was a wooden slatted hut with a tin roof. His flip flops flipped and flopped with each step as he went.

I could hear German accents, Dutch accents, a group of Aussies playing a drinking game raucously at another one of the tables on the beach itself and an English accent from a woman sat behind me, as she ordered a Jack Daniels and Coke with a twist of lime.

I recognised the voice instantly, and I'd only ever heard one person order that drink before. It couldn't be. Could it? Of all the cafes in all the world, and she happens to have walked into mine?

I tried to turn nonchalantly, not easy when you are as big as Mark Vickers and squeezed into a little plastic chair.

I now sided on to the woman who was partially hidden behind a book and large sunglasses as well as covered with an oversized straw hat.

But there was no mistaking that it was her. I'd heard the voice a thousand times, ordered that drink for her on countless occasions, woken up next to her, so many times, and here she was sat in the same beachside café, half a world away from where we had first met outside KFC. My heart was pounding. Here she was, right next to me.

Fucking Nikki.

In hindsight, I started talking to her out of morbid curiosity. Curiosity and wanting to gloat about the money a bit maybe. I hoped of all hope that she still lived in the flat in High Wycombe next to Lidl that she'd bought with the proceeds of our house.

"Oh, you're English?" I said in Nikki's direction.

I saw her weigh me up in the few seconds before she answered.

"Yep, I sure am," she said, with a disinterested smile that used the minimal amount of facial muscles. She didn't bother to lower the book she was reading. The fashionably tatty t-shirt was doing the trick.

"Whereabouts are you from?" I asked.

Nikki sighed almost inaudibly.

"Just outside London," she said, making it clear that her reading material held far more interest than a conversation with me.

"Cool, I'm from a bit further out. Crappy town in Buckinghamshire. High Wycombe? You've probably passed it on your way up the M40. Couldn't wait to get away!" I replied, turning away slightly and picking up my Coke. I could see her looking at me out of the corner of my eye, trying to decide the best way to respond.

"Yeah, I know it," she finally said, before returning to her book.

I peeled myself from my chair and stood, square on Nikki's eye line but looking over her head towards the café.

"I wonder how long that toastie will be? I could eat my own leg," I said, putting my foot up on my chair to retighten a lace on my trainer and at the same time showing off my huge calf muscle, and shorts stretching thighs. I saw her notice.

"Can you do me a favour?" I asked, peeling off my T-shirt and letting her see the rest of the merchandise. I subtly flexed all of my muscles from the arms like tree trunks to abs like a bag of shrink-wrapped tennis balls. She lowered her book, ever so slightly. "Can you watch my stuff, I just realised I left my wallet in my car?" I chucked my t-shirt over the back of my chair and walked past her, not bothering to wait for an answer.

I'd deliberately parked the Lamborghini where I would be able to see it from the beach, and as I walked towards it, was as grateful for that as I had been for virtually anything else in my life. My wallet was, of course, already in my pocket, however, I trotted around the car to the boot from where I could see that Nikki had turned in her seat and was looking in my direction. I opened the boot of the Lamborghini and was now hidden from her. Obligatory fist pump.

As I closed the boot, I saw Nikki turn back quickly before flicking through a few of the pages of her book.

"Thanks," I said, retaking my seat, facing away from Nikki and towards the ocean. I stretched out my long legs and interlaced my fingers behind my head just as the child waiter was flip-flopping towards me with a limp looking toastie and Nikki's JD and Coke with lime.

"So, are you just here for a holiday or are you travelling around?" came Nikki's voice from behind me. More animated this time.

"I'm travelling around actually, was in Sri Lanka before this and heading off to Vietnam next, I think. Depends where the wind blows me. I have a little boat moored off Phuket. What about you?"

"Yeah, I'm just going with the flow, you never what's gonna happen next, do you? That's why I love travelling."

"No, you fucking don't!" I blurted.

Nikki froze in her seat before putting her drink on the table in front of her.

"I'm sorry?" she said, scared and confused.

'Shit!' I thought.

"No, you fucking don't," I said again less aggressively before reaching across and swiping an imaginary bug from Nikki's table.

"Little bugger was about to crawl into your crisps! Bloody insects." And proceeded to swat a non-existent fly off my arm.

"Thank you," Nikki said cautiously, lifting the opening to the crisp packet on her table and peaking inside.

She hated travelling when we were together. I couldn't even get her to go to Bournemouth for the bloody day.

I took a bite of the toastie that tasted far better than it looked.

"Nice car," Nikki said, nodding towards the Lambo.

"Yeah, it's rented but it's the same as one I have at home. Only in yellow not red. Will probably get shot of it actually, a bit tight on the legroom."

"I bet you find that a lot don't you, you are very... big," she put the straw to her drink in her mouth and stared at me over the top of her sunglasses as she sucked.

"Yes, yes, I am," I tried to say provocatively but, on taking another bite of toastie, left a long piece of tomato hanging out of my mouth that I had to manhandle back in.

'*Sexy*' I thought.

"So, wife's back on the boat?" Nikki said conversationally as if the answer was of no concern.

"Nope, just little old me. I was married, bitch cheated on me," I said taking another bite of the sandwich.

"Her loss though, I came into the money not long after the divorce came through." I watched her face for any sign of recognition, any twinkling of guilt. Nothing.

"Honestly, whatever happened to 'death do us part' eh?" Nikki said without any hint of irony as I choked on a piece of a toastie and proceeded to have a coughing fit.

Fortunately for both of us, nearly dying at the hands of the chunk of bread prevented me from dragging her across the beach and drowning her in the sea.

As I sat there recovering, red-faced, sweating, covered in my own saliva, I realised that no amount of money or good looks would ever make me any 'cooler'.

Nikki was unperturbed however and kept asking the right questions, making impressed sounds at the right times, fiddling with the hair that hung down from under her hat and giggling like a teenager at appropriate times. It wasn't the first time I'd been on the other end of her flirting and to be fair, she was pretty good at it. It didn't stop me fantasising about throwing her in the Ocean occasionally, however.

She talked, I pretended to give a shit and a few more drinks were consumed. Every now and then I'd be reminded of why I fell in love with her. These thoughts were easily pushed aside by also remembering how she and her arsehole solicitor managed to leave me with no furniture and only enough of our joint account to do a week's shopping. She was likely travelling the world on her percentage four years later.

Long shadows were being cast across the beach now as the sun dropped behind palm trees, its reflection on the sea almost too bright to look at. Nikki was saying something about what a free spirit she was and how she always tried to say 'yes' to things nowadays. All I could think about was how much Jo would have loved the light.

We'd sometimes sit in my garden in Vegas, and she would try and take pictures of the sunsets on her phone, always frustrated that it never looked quite as good as the real thing. She had hundreds of sunsets on her phone, each one very slightly different and could never bring herself to delete any of them.

I decided it was time to go in for the kill and seal the deal.

"Here, wanna see a picture of my little boat? I didn't actually have a photo of my Yacht on my phone, but fortunately, there were several dozen of it on Google."

"Here you go," I said, stretching across and handing Nikki my phone.

"Good God!" Nikki said, taking off her sunglasses and shaking her head at the screen. "This is yours?"

I took the phone back and looked at the picture myself.

"Yep, it's got everything I need. And some other stuff."

"Wow. I'd love to see it," she said, looking me in the eye, taking off her hat and flicking her hair over one shoulder.

Despite everything, I am still a red-blooded male, and I won't pretend it didn't occur to me to take her back to the boat and do the deed for old time's sake. I let myself remember how I'd felt stood on that landing that day and how I'd felt closing the front door on our home for the last time.

"Sounds like a great idea," I said. "I'll give you the grand tour, I'll call ahead, and they can get us some food together maybe? The chef is amaaazing!"

"Awesome!" Nikki said, shuffling her belongings together on the table.

"Perhaps some champagne on the deck, just see where the night takes us?" I said with a wink.

"Sounds like a plan," Nikki said, winking back.

I stood as she started quickly dumping everything she had into a beach bag that was hanging on the back of her chair. The coincidence of meeting her here was ludicrous. I'd once bumped into an ex-girlfriend in Sports Direct in Milton Keynes but nothing like this.

Maybe it was the 'choice' the Monk had mentioned? Maybe I was being tested in some way? Maybe I was being observed to see how much I'd grown, the spiritual awakening from my time in Sri Lanka being carefully examined?

We walked to my car. I decided to jump over the driver's door and slide into the cockpit as Nikki walked around and tried to open the other door. She could barely contain her excitement and looked so pleased with herself I thought she might explode.

I started the car as she pulled at the handle time and time again. She looked at me confused as I revved the engine and remembered Dave on my landing holding my 'World's Best Husband' mug.

I spun the wheels on the dusty ground and reversed the Lamborghini around a dazed Nikki until she was level with my door.

"Fuck you, Nikki. Fuck you!"

I raced the car out of the car park covering Nikki in grit and dust as she grew smaller in my rear-view mirror. Not deliberate but something I did chuckle to myself about that evening whilst sipping champagne on the top deck of my yacht, feet up on the railings and watching the rippling reflection of the moon on the water. Was I proud of my actions? No. Had it been petty? Probably. Satisfying? Definitely.

Chapter 13

I was showering the next morning when I became aware that the engines were rumbling, and we were soon to be leaving the waters of Thailand for our next destination. Vietnam had been somewhere I'd wanted to go since I was a small boy flicking through the exotic travel brochures in Lunn Poly whilst my dad booked our annual trip to Menorca. It always looked like a different Planet to me.

I stepped dripping from the shower, pulled a towel from the rail and started to dry my hair. I dragged the towel down my face and opened my eyes.

"For the love of God, you have got to stop doing that!" I shouted at Juan, who was standing leaning against the door frame of the en-suite bathroom.

Suddenly aware of my nakedness, I dropped the towel to my mid-region and pushed past him into the bedroom.

"Just came to check all is OK after your little meeting with Nikki yesterday? That was my idea. You're welcome by the way."

"Didn't think it was just a bizarre coincidence. Thanks, I suppose. Feel a bit dirty about the whole thing today but hey, she deserved it," I said drying myself quickly and hunting around for some underwear.

"Oh, you know, old wounds and all that. I thought the wheel spin was a nice touch by the way."

"I didn't mean to do that. The clutches on those things are really sensitive." I pulled some boxer shorts on whilst managing to maintain my discretion and sat in a chair.

"Quite a close call though, at the end of the day you made contact with her first, and you know the rules," Juan said wagging his finger at me with raised eyebrows.

"Hang on a second, that's… that's what do you call it? Entrapment? Yeah, entrapment. You lot putting her there for me to 'happen to bump into'."

"It was all me. Head office had no idea. Just thought we owed you one. Caught the bosses off guard too. One in forty-four thousand, three hundred and fifty-eight apparently. The chances of you two meeting there coincidentally. But they bought it. You had a lucky escape though. Consequences remember," Juan said, rifling through cupboards looking for the fridge.

"So your little 'revenge gift' to me nearly got me in trouble? Thanks for that, and if you are looking for the fridge, I had it removed. Was too easy to snack before bed every night."

Juan looked disappointed and perched himself on the end of the bed.

"So you didn't come to check if I was OK but to warn me about the rules again. Is that right?"

"Bit of both I suppose. The big bosses thought you needed a little refresher, and I wanted to check you weren't moping around your room listening to Morrisey."

We arrived in the waters off Vietnam that evening, Juan having spent the day in the pool and chatting up the female crew members, me googling everything I wanted to see and do when we went ashore.

Toni joined us for dinner, I enjoyed her company, and it meant less time having to talk to Juan by myself.

At the end of the meal, Juan stood up and thanked Toni and I for our company and for a 'cracking bit of grub'. He looked back at me one last time before disappearing into the boat.

"Just be careful Mark, yeah? They won't allow any more close calls."

He tapped the side of his head with his index finger. *'Think'*.

As I expected when I awoke the next day, Juan was gone.

Vietnam was everything I'd hoped it would be, and I ended up staying for almost three months. I joined guided walking tours, hiked deep into the countryside with other intrepid travellers and befriended backpackers from all over the world in some of the most unexpected places. I had learned quickly to hide all signs of my wealth or people rarely wanted to talk about anything else.

It was the company I enjoyed the most. Before I'd met Jo in Vegas, in Dubai and even on the boat, there were so many nights of eating alone. Although I'd had many, many evenings with acquaintances, even some people I'd call friends, it was outweighed by those spent by myself, at first in Michelin star restaurants but eventually and predominantly at the kitchen counter of the house or yacht, hoping to start a conversation with a member of the staff or crew.

I had learned the hard way that a meaningful relationship wasn't possible and would just lead to more hurt. Even friendships had a shelf life. That was the beauty of my time in Vietnam. Although my time with people was never more than a few days or a couple of weeks as, ultimately, everyone was just passing through, people were far more open, more honest about their fallibilities and shortcomings, hopes and dreams.

More compassionate than the people I'd spent my time with in Vegas. Perhaps that's something to do with the mindset of the traveller. You need to forge strong bonds with people quickly. Giving and receiving empathy is crucial. You never know when you might want to cadge a lift or share a Pot Noodle. I spent more and more time on land and less and less time on the Yacht.

But it wasn't just my fellow travellers. The Vietnamese people never ceased to surprise me with their generosity, even when they had very little to give.

Towards the end of my time there, feeling overly confident whilst trekking with a South African guy I'd met a few days before, I persuaded him that I knew a better route back to a hostel he was staying at, than the map he had paid good money for.

We took my 'shortcut' whilst making our way through some farmland that I was convinced I had walked before.

Several hours later, my South African walking partner having stopped talking to me sometime earlier, I admitted defeat. I was pretty sure the path we were treading between two rice fields was the same one we had walked many hours before. I apologised to Peter for the tenth time and slumped down onto a rock, tired and hungry.

The temptation to call the Yacht and have them send me a helicopter was almost overwhelming. I even took my phone out of my rucksack and unlocked the screen. No signal. Of course.

In a far corner of the field, a man was hunched over with some sort of tool, working on an area of ground. I left Peter, emptying his bag, frantically looking for something to eat and made my way across the field.

I'd picked up some of the basic languages whilst there and was able to say 'Xin Cao', which was 'hello' and 'Cho xin bia', beer, please. But not much more. My pidgin Spanish hadn't got me very far and I'd had the most success with my GCSE French.

I approached the man slowly, and he stood up from his work, tipping his non-la, his wide-brimmed bamboo hat, back off his brow. It was keeping the man almost completely shaded from the sun. He appeared to be perhaps sixty years old, weathered by many years of toil, possibly only ever in this very field.

"Do you speak English?" I said.

The man shrugged.

"Parlez Vous Francais?" I tried.

"Oui," the man replied.

I unfolded the map I was holding and showed it to the farmer.

"Ville? Ici? *Town*? *Here*?" was the best I could come up with and moved my finger frantically around the map.

"Tu es la," he said, pointing to a green area on the map. I worked out this meant 'you are here' and that it was so far from where we were supposed to be, I wouldn't have the bottle to tell Peter.

The man must have seen my shoulders drop and said something else I didn't understand. I pointed to where we were supposed to be and, defeated, dropped my bag into the mud.

The man nodded to himself and reached past me, picking my bag up and throwing it over his shoulder. It was almost as big as him.

"Suivez moi, suivez moi!" he said, motioning for me to follow him. Having not a huge amount of options, one of them being dying of exposure in a Vietnamese rainforest, I didn't bother protesting, instead of hollering across the field at Peter to pick up his shit and join me.

We followed the man across three identical fields, at which point I realised the naivety of me trying to navigate this beautiful but vast landscape on my own.

Eventually, we reached what was no more than a wooden hut on stilts, perhaps half the size of my bathroom on the yacht.

The entire place was now in the shade of a mountain, the foot at which, the house was nestled amongst what appeared to be Mango trees.

The word 'idyllic' popped into my head as we approached the house, and I found myself strangely jealous. It did cross my mind that I could probably buy the entire area, and in fact the mountain itself, for a fraction of the cost of the yacht I was living on.

A woman, of similar age to the farmer, was sat stirring a pot that was hung over a smoking fire. He said something to her as we approached, and she responded kindly and with a smile, although to be fair, they could have been saying,

"Found two more of these morons in a field, we are gonna need a bigger pot, the big one will last us months!"

I hoped not though.

The woman nodded and smiled at us, and we reciprocated.

I could see an old Citroen C5 parked next to a fenced-off area containing chickens.

"I take, I take!" the farmer said, nodding towards the car.

I took this to mean he would take us to the nearest town and was so grateful I collapsed to my knees and laughed.

"Merci Beaucoup, merci beaucoup," I said, pressing my hands together as if in prayer. We were exhausted.

Peter even managed to smile at me as he rested on his rucksack.

I remembered suddenly that I had spent the last of my cash buying us bottles of water from a roadside stall some hours before and was certain he wasn't able to take my platinum credit card as payment.

"No money," I said apologetically, pulling the material from my empty shorts pockets out to emphasise the point.

The man looked as if I had told him I was planning on violating his wife and defecating in his dinner.

"Non," he said angrily, waving his finger at me "Non." At first, I thought he was refusing to take us without payment but then it dawned on me that he was offended by my suggestion of payment.

"Thank you," I said again. "Merci, merci."

He nodded and showed us to a small table next to the fire.

The woman, whom I assumed was his wife, removed the pot from the fire and placed it on the ground. I could now see what appeared to be rice, pieces of chicken and a green leaf of some description. It looked barely enough for one, never mind both of them.

The man placed two cups of water in front of Peter and I and poured two more for himself and his wife. The smell wafting up from the pot was making my stomach rumble, my last stick of Kit Kat having been eaten about three hours previously. I saw Peter craning to have a look at the pot's contents also.

I saw the old woman place four bowls on the floor.

"No!" I said. "Yours. We are OK." The entire contents of the pot would have been about the size of a starter chef would prepare for me on the yacht and a lift to town was already more than we could have asked for. Peter was equally adamant, thanking them profusely in French and English and even Afrikaans, but insisting. Neither of us wanted these people to go hungry.

The old woman waved us away, again saying something GCSE French wasn't adequate for and spooned the steaming hot food into the four bowls equally. The man had been working in the field all day and no doubt his wife had worked equally hard to ensure they had enough to survive. In sharing their food with us, they would almost certainly be going hungry themselves.

The man put the bowls down in front of us with an indignant *thump,* but a friendly smile. Peter and I weren't ignorant to the fact that continuing to argue would have just caused more offence and gratefully got stuck into the food in front of us. It was the most generous act I had ever witnessed.

We finished our meals and the old man fired up the C5. It wasn't going to be as comfortable a ride as the Lambo, but the farmer climbed in with enough confidence to suggest it would get us to where we needed to go.

We said our goodbyes to the farmer's wife and bounced off down a dirt track in the tiny car, our rucksacks on our laps and at least a little food in our bellies. I kept thinking about what the farmer and his wife had given us and pondered if I had ever done anything half as selfless in my life? I decided I probably hadn't.

Twenty minutes later we were in a town I recognised as somewhere I had stayed a month or so before. I thanked the farmer for the hundredth time as I gingerly closed the car door, half expecting it to come off in my hand. I leaned in the passenger window and thanked him again.

I wanted to make sure I remembered the man's face, promising myself I would find a way of repaying him one day. He nodded to me and waved out of the window as he turned in the road and headed for home.

"What now?" Peter asked, with us still being nowhere near to the place he was staying.

"Now we find the most expensive hotel we can, shower, stuff our faces, get really drunk and sleep like logs," I said, pulling out the Platinum credit card I had first held in Las Vegas almost eighteen months before.

Peter looked first at me, then at the credit card, then back at me, resisted any urge to protest and spoke.

"Yeah. Okay then."

Chapter 14

As much as I had fallen in love with Vietnam and its people, it was a big world I still had to try and get around, and I wanted to cover as much of it on the yacht being skippered by Toni as I could.

The plan was to stop off in the Philippines before heading North to Hong Kong and Japan. From there, I wanted to hit New Zealand and spend a reasonable amount of time travelling down the East Coast of Australia that Toni talked about so much. 'God's country' she called it.

I was wondering what sort of bonus I could give Toni when her contract ended that wouldn't change her life but show how grateful I was for her help and company. She had become a friend during my time on the yacht, and I would miss her when Mark Vickers time was up. And then something occurred to me. For a few moments, my conscience battled with my inert selfishness but not for long I am proud to say.

I picked up my phone and called Toni down from the bridge. I was on the pool deck at the time, reading the eighth Lee Child book of my cruise. With my current size and stature, I fancied myself a bit of a Jack Reacher. Only less brave and more shit at fighting.

"Sir, yes sir!" she smiled and saluted as she walked towards me.

"We're going the wrong way. I've decided to change course."

"Okaaay..." Toni said pensively but respectfully.

"Yeah, I'm gonna sack off Hong Kong and Japan. We'll stop for one night off the Philippines and then head straight to Oz."

"We've already arranged all the permits for Hong Kong," Toni started, doing a reasonable job of hiding some annoyance at how flaky I was being with her schedule, "And it was a bit of a nightmare getting the paperwork done for Okinawa, we can't just rock up in something this size. Your shout, Mark, but there are some incredible things to see up there, and it's a long trek back up later, particularly if we want to head across to Peru after like we discussed?"

"Nope, I've made my mind up. We are going to get down to Brisbane as soon as possible and push you overboard so you can be with your husband and daughter. All I ask is that you find me a Skipper half as good as you who can also make a decent Mojito. I'll pay you up to the end of your contract, but you can spend the rest of it with your family," I sincerely hoped this was against any 'rules'.

Toni stood speechless. She was a hard-nosed Aussie whom I'd witnessed first-hand verbally take down senior officials at some of the places we'd moored up on our journey, especially if she thought they were taking the piss with their required 'payments'. But on this occasion, she was genuinely lost for words. She still had six months on her contract and wouldn't otherwise see her daughter until the end of that time. Another six months of growing up she would miss.

I have no doubt she battled with the idea of arguing with me, even if just for obligatory reasons, but as she stood there looking at me, 'gob smacked' as she described it later, all I saw was reddening in the eyes and clenching of her jaw. I felt a lump in my own throat seeing her like that, very un-Jack-Reacher-like I thought, stood and hugged her into me, as much to hide any potential leakage from the eye region as it was for her benefit. Toni being Toni, allowed this sentimental nonsense for about five seconds before pushing me away and straightening her uniform.

I'd miss her, but the feeling I had been able to do that for her was greater than any joy I'd experienced as Mark Vickers. Possibly ever.

The new Captain was no Toni but an excellent substitute, a bear of a Welshman that Toni said would keep me in check and whom she had crewed with before becoming a Captain herself. He certainly knew his stuff, and his stories from his time in the Royal Navy kept me entertained as we crisscrossed the world's oceans.

We did head back up towards the Far East after Toni went ashore and the contrast between Tokyo and the villages of Vietnam and temples of Sri Lanka, made you question whether you were still on the same planet.

From there, we sailed South East for the Americas. What I was effectively doing was taking a route I had mainly planned on backpacking with a mate when I was eighteen. On that occasion, I had taken a job at a local bookie's, the idea being to save every penny and purchase around the world open plane ticket. Three months in, however, I had saved no money at all and owed my dad forty-six quid. The dream died in the bottom of a beer glass in the pub at the bottom of my road.

There was a lot to be said about 'backpacking' from a Super Yacht with a Cinema room, squash court and its own driving range, so maybe these things happen for a reason.

I was driving golf balls off the rear deck of the yacht, approximately three hundred nautical miles West of Chile. I felt my stomach rumble and wondered how long it was until lunch was served. On most days, I would eat breakfast at my leisure and the head waiter would ask what time I would like to dine for lunch that day.

I looked at my watch to see if we were approaching grub time as it rolled down another day:

'0 6 3'

Just over two months to go.

The watch was a ticking time bomb on my wrist. I had no idea where I would be, or who I would be, sixty-four days from now.

It was a cruel part of the game. As with my last weeks in Vegas, the apprehension of what was coming served to sap the enjoyment from the remaining time. I'd seen and done some incredible things like Marcus and Mark but I had also lost Jo, lied to friends about who I was, left my homes, in Roquetas and Vegas and had to live with the knowledge that I had no concept of what physical or spiritual price I was ultimately going to pay for the privilege of being able to stand and slice golf balls off the back of a giant boat into the South Pacific Ocean.

The puppet show in which I was the main protagonist was being choreographed by a cruel, cruel Director. I wondered briefly if Diego was now being whipped by the flames of Hell or seeing out his time as a poor man in Spain, no better off than the day he received the watch and doomed to live out these days fretting over what was next.

I pondered on how long a person could live as I was, with no lasting connection to other human beings, no shared experiences to laugh about, shared memories with friends in years to come, nowhere to call home. No love.

I spotted a Gull bobbing up and down in the wake of the boat, perhaps a hundred yards away. Placing a golf ball angrily onto the plastic tee at my feet, I imagined the Gull was Juan, the smiling assassin. Pretending to be my friend but ultimately just an agent of whatever evil held my fate in its hand.

I had nothing against Gulls and knew full well my golf game would put it in no danger whatsoever. However, having made a rare and clean connection on the ball, it plopped into the ocean a matter of feet from the bird, causing it to squawk and take flight.

"Sorry, mate!" I shouted as it flapped its way into the clear blue sky and soared over my head.

I slumped onto a sun lounger.

Captain Andy joined me for dinner and managed to cheer me up with a story about a pretty girl he met in Thailand whom it later emerged had larger testicles than he did. In the story, he discovered this before things reached the point of no return, but I wasn't so sure.

A plan began to formulate in my mind that I would spend my last days as Mark Vickers walking the Inca Trail, ideally reaching the majesty of Machu Picchu on my last day. It seemed suitably apt and an appropriate end to this part of my journey. I felt I'd earned the right to be a little cliched and at the end of the day, who was going to know?

We moored up off the coast of Chile the next morning.

I had someone arrange flights for me between the countries, right the way up through Central America. Honduras, Ecuador, Panama. Costa Rica, with its natural beauty and peaceful way of life, became somewhere I swore I would return to and spend more time in the future.

I tried desperately to submerge myself in the *real* South America but occasionally the temptation of a five-star hotel, rainfall shower, Emperor bed and even the odd Casino, was too much for me. I became slightly frantic in those last few weeks as Mark, suddenly extremely aware of the watch weighing heavy on my wrist.

I choppered back to the Yacht and had what he didn't realise was our last beer, with Captain Andy. I'd miss the boat and assumed I'd probably buy another at some point. Decisions, decisions, although the purchase of another Jet was top of my current shopping list.

I'd been told that hiking the Inca trail takes about four days but the thought of not reaching its iconic conclusion made me allow an extra day. I set off with the counter on the watch reading:

'0 0 5'

I walked as part of a group and spent those days chatting to people from all over the world and of all backgrounds. They told an inspiring array of stories. Some funny, some

175

shocking and some sad. In our group of ten people, there were young backpackers, middle-aged businessmen on spiritual journeys, trying to escape the futility of the rat race and even a retired couple who had been planning the trip for thirty years. As usual, I had to be suitably vague when asked a question and had a hard time explaining why I never bothered taking any photos.

On the afternoon of the fourth day, we reached the Sun Gate on Machu Picchu Mountain. The mist was sat sporadically on the canopy of the forest below us and the lateness of the hour was creating complex shadows stretching away from the ancient ruins.

I sat on a low flat rock and tried to take in everything I was seeing, to absorb the view as much as possible for fear of never being here again. Feeling justifiably melancholy, I began to reflect on the previous year of my life. The first few months had been largely tainted by the grief of losing Jo and in quiet times I still missed her so much my chest hurt.

But later there had been moments of joy and epiphany, even shame, however, as I remembered leaving Nikki in a cloud of dust in the car park in Thailand. As much as I had enjoyed driving away on that day, I couldn't help but feel I had given up my enviable position on the moral high ground. I recalled Mr Nguyen, the Vietnamese farmer and his wife and Peter who I had dragged across the countryside until we had run out of food and water, Rosh, my jolly Sri Lankan guide, and the Monk who inexplicably seemed to know my story. I hoped I would see them all again one day.

As I lay in my tent on the eve of my last day, trillionaire Mark Vickers using his bag as a pillow, I drifted away imagining taking Jo to meet all of those people one day. And slept a peaceful sleep.

Chapter 15

I woke early on the last day, the canvass of the tent giving precious little protection from the bright morning sun. This brought back memories of my first two 'transitions' and at first I thought I'd morphed into my new persona early. After a brief panic and gradual realisation that I'd just forgotten to put my silk, lavender-infused eye-mask on the previous evening (I always swore money wouldn't change me) I crawled from the tent. The ruins looked completely different at that time of day, and I was grateful to have been able to see them at both.

Whereas in the evening they had appeared haunting and almost mystical, this morning it was easy to imagine them bustling with life all those years ago before the Spanish rocked up and either murdered them or gave them some disease they had no immunity to. I stood, stretched my ample frame and imagined market traders preparing for the day, Women washing clothes on stone slabs, the odd Human sacrifice. Just another Friday for your ordinary Inca.

As we reached mid-morning and my group began to pack up their belongings, I found myself in a heated argument with our guide about why I wasn't returning with the group. He was shouting half in English and half in

Spanish about Insurance and losing his job, and at the point, he realised he wasn't going to get me back down that mountain and was on the verge of tears, I put my arm around him and walked him away from the gathering crowd.

"Senor, I am sorry about the trouble that this will cause you. Hopefully, this will help?" I said, pulling what I knew to be about three months wages from my wallet and pushing it down into the front pocket of his jacket.

"Si Senor, this will help greatly," he said grinning. "Enjoy your extra day with the Incas!"

I spent the day walking and reading the book the businessman from Canada had finished and handed me the day before, '*The art of happiness*' by *his Holiness the Dalai Lama*. Not my usual thing, I was more of a guns and kidnapping and government conspiracies type of guy, but it was all the reading material I had left, and it seemed fitting in some way.

My mind wandered to where I might be this time tomorrow. Monaco? Paris? New York maybe? I checked the watch. 7:42 p.m.

"It's heavy going but sticks with it, the section on 'Suffering' is a bit depressing but there's some good stuff."

I was sat on the ground on my extremely expensive, now grass-stained, sweater and had to shield my eyes with my hand against the sun that was now sitting low in the sky. With the light so bright behind her, she was just a dark figure.

A dark figure with an English accent.

"Sorry," she said, seeing me squinting up at her before shuffling ninety degrees to my left. "Didn't mean to blind you. I read it in an airport last year in one sitting. Wasn't supposed to, bloody delays, eh?"

The woman half turned and lifted her camera to her face before snapping what will have been the sun setting behind the ruins.

She'd always had a great eye for framing a photo. A picture she'd taken on our trip to the Grand Canyon was blown up and hung in the hallway of the Vegas house.

Jo.

I couldn't move. I couldn't speak. I had quite literally no idea what to do at that instant. My vision narrowed to a pinprick, and I realised I wasn't breathing.

"Oh, sorry," she said after several seconds of me staring at her blankly, "I thought you spoke English." And pointed to the book.

"And I am still speaking, and you still don't know what I am saying."

With that, she rolled her eyes at her own mistake, smiled, and turned to walk away.

"Wait!" I managed to squeeze out from somewhere in the depths of my consciousness. Some part of me knew that I needed to emit words to stop her from leaving.

"I do speak English. *Am* English," I said, scrabbling to my feet, getting myself caught up in my jacket and almost falling flat on my face.

"Careful," she said, putting her hand out instinctively and catching my arm as I stumbled forward.

Her expression changed instantly, and she recoiled as if she'd had some sort of electric shock.

"Are you OK?" I said with genuine concern, her smile replaced with a furrowed brow and curling and uncurling of her fingers.

"Erm, yeah…yep, I'm fine. Just had the strangest feeling," she said slowly, still distracted by the feeling in her hand. "Must be the altitude."

I relied on the very basics of conversation to buy me some time while I decided what to do and fought the urge to scoop her up and kiss her until my lips fell off. It was Jo. Here. Stood in front of me, large as life and twice as beautiful.

"I'm Mike. Mark, I mean. I'm Mark. My middle name is Mike. Mark Michael Vickers, that's me."

"Hi Mark Michael, I'm Jo," she said with a friendly, mocking tone but with a whisper of memory from one of the first times we met, tapping at a door in her mind. '...not Mike. Marcus. Just Marcus'

My heart was pounding out of my chest, and I knew right then that if I didn't try and explain to her what was happening, what had *happened*, I'd regret it until the day I died. I didn't care why she was there, who had put her there, there was every likelihood I was completely fucked anyway so what did it matter?

Screw Juan.

Screw whoever his boss was.

Telling her or not telling her didn't feel like any kind of choice as we stood on top of that Mountain, me barely able to force air in and out of my lungs and her looking dazed and confused.

The time frame worked. It had been a year since I'd seen her last and based on her long-term plans of spending another twelve months travelling North and South America, that we had discussed doing together at some point actually, perhaps this was also the conclusion of that journey for her. Regardless, there was simply no way this was a chance meeting. Someone somewhere had decided to put a sick little twist at the end of the script.

I was certain this was the choice the Monk had spoken to me about. Don't tell her and everything carries on as normal, (or as normal as things get around here) or tell her and suffer 'consequences'.

Which was the 'right' choice? I had no idea. All I knew was that the woman I loved, the woman I'd thought about every day for the last year, imagined being with, spending my life with, was standing three feet away from me on the top of a mountain in Peru, and I was due to 'transition' at some point in the next few hours. You had to admit 'They' had a sense of humour.

A thought suddenly crashed into my mind that made my blood run cold, and I instantly felt sweat starting to bead all over my body.

"Are you here by yourself?" I asked, looking around for travel companions, or worse still, companions.

"Yep, here with everyone I can rely on," Jo laughed but there was a darkness to the comment. I immediately felt guilty as she raised the camera again.

I couldn't stop looking at her. Her hair, the curve of her chin, the way she always stood with one hand on her hip, were so familiar to me and not just reaching out and touching her seemed like it would take more strength than I had.

But I didn't know how long I had left. Adrenalin was coursing through me, and I knew it was now or never.

I also knew that how I tried to explain this would be the difference between her falling into my arms in floods of tears or running down the mountain screaming about the crazy man.

"Jo," I started. "This is going to sound strange, but we know each other."

She brought the camera down again and let it hang around her neck on its strap, before turning back to me with a quizzical, half-smile and looking at me as if trying to solve a puzzle.

"Have we? Did we meet in Mexico on that donkey trek? No, I can't imagine you getting on a donkey actually," she said looking me up and down.

"No, it wasn't in Mexico. It was in Vegas."

I was trying to stay calm and collected, arranging my thoughts before letting them enter the world and potentially wreaking havoc.

Jo looked doubtful.

"Oh, okay. You'd struggle to get two more different places," she said turning and surveying the vast and lush green landscape enveloping us. I nodded.

"Hmm... at the restaurant?" Jo asked.

"Actually, that was where we first met. But it wasn't the last. Look, I'm really sorry, I know this is going to sound weird, but can I tell you a story? It will make everything clear, no more believable, but at least you will know everything. I'll try and make it quick?"

I'd obviously failed to deliver that in a way that reassured Jo, and she simply stood with a concerned look on her face.

"I know you don't remember me, but I remember you, I remember that you are from just outside London and decided to travel after your husband died, kind of as a pilgrimage for him. I know your mum had some sort of accident a year or so ago. But is OK now?" I asked tentatively, far from sure Juan had been truthful with me.

I could see Jo trying to work out who I was, how I knew these things, perhaps even a little embarrassed that she didn't remember me despite the fact that we had clearly spent some time talking at some point.

"Yes," she replied. "My mum's fine."

"You might wanna sit down," I said, trying to sound light and breezy but managing to make it sound like I was about to tell Jo that her dog had been hit by a car.

I dragged my sweater across for her to sit on which she did. Curiosity getting the better of her.

I started telling Jo about being sat in a bar in Spain one evening, two years ago. I told her an abridged version of the story Diego had told me.

"I'm going to need you to keep a REALLY open mind for this next bit," I said.

She was certainly intrigued so far at least, and sat listening, asking the occasional question which I answered if I could.

I explained that I had fallen asleep in my crappy little apartment in Roquetas De Mar and woken up in the Penthouse Suite of the Palazzo Hotel in Las Vegas. I paused and watched her face for a reaction. Just a small nod.

I explained about Juan, about going to her restaurant to write a list of all the things I could do and buy. I explained how I never did get around to buying the Giraffe. She didn't laugh.

At this point, I hadn't said *who* I was.

I explained that she served me and my 'friend' that he had told me about her two jobs and her work in the community up in the old part of Vegas.

Still, I couldn't find the words to tell her who I was.

It was getting dark and the moon rising in the sky took on the shape of a noose in my mind.

It was impossible to tell what Jo was thinking. Her expression could have been confusion, disbelief, bewilderment, concern for my mental health even. I just didn't know, and so ploughed on.

I explained that we spoke briefly in the restaurant as we were both from England but then I got really drunk and had to be taken back to the Hotel.

I knew I was reaching the crux of it. So far, I could have been one of a hundred people whom she'd served at the restaurant. But once I told her about our second meeting, at the party where she served me in the marquee, the cat would be out of the bag.

"Marcus," she suddenly said. "You are saying you are Marcus? Marcus Taylor? That's how I met him."

Again, words completely failed me. I was terrified that if I simply answered 'yes' she would run off and I'd never see her again.

Hearing her say that name again made my throat close up, and I just wanted to hold her. Hold her and sob into her and never, ever, let her go again.

"Look, before you say anything else, I know how all this sounds, how all this looks," I said, spreading my arms and showing what was an unfamiliar body to her.

Jo ran her hands through her hair and sighed.

"So, what you are saying, is that you are the reincarnation of my ex-boyfriend, who, not only left me when I needed him the most, and disappeared off the face of the Earth by the way, but that you also just happened to be here, in Peru, on this Mountain when I was? Just so I'm clear of course."

I tried to think of a way of responding that made it sound less ridiculous. But I couldn't.

"Yep. That's pretty much it."

Legs crossed on my sweater, Jo leaned back on her hands and laughed.

"Now, I've heard some pretty amazing stories while I've been travelling around, there was even a guy in Honduras who claimed to be the reincarnation of his dad's goat, but that's by far the best. Bravo," she said with a sarcastic clap.

"What I want to know pal before I have you arrested for harassment, is how the Hell do you know all that stuff about how I met Marcus and what is it you actually think you are going to get out of this?"

Tears were forming in the corner of her eyes. She would always cry when she was angry. Which would make her more angry.

"I need you to hear me out. I can't leave this place without you *knowing* what happened. For your sake, not mine. Have me arrested, push me off the mountain if you want to, I don't care anymore, but let me finish. If you want

186

to walk away at the end of it and put me down as some crackpot, then fine. But give me ten minutes. Please?"

As I finished, I looked at my watch. Perhaps to make a mental note of when this theoretical ten minutes was starting, perhaps to confirm for the hundredth time that day that this was indeed the last few hours as Mark Vickers. Perhaps just to check the time.

Whatever it was, it changed everything.

"Where did you get Marcus's watch?"

Of course. Jo had seen me wear that unique, gold, diamond-encrusted, 'El Diablo' watch, every day of our time together.

"Yes!" I exclaimed excitedly. "The watch, *my* watch!"

I hurriedly removed it from my wrist and handed it across to Jo.

She turned it over and over in her fingers. She looked at me, then back at the watch, then back at me.

As she examined the watch and wrestled with the myriad thoughts and theories that must have been bombarding her brain at that point, I started speaking again. I told her how on my first day as Marcus Taylor I had woken up with a different body, a different face, I'd woken a different person. I told her about the 'laws', about how I'd always wanted to donate more to the shelter, but it was forbidden for me to give 'life-changing' amounts of money away.

I told her about that last day in Vegas, the texts, the voicemails, the mania with which I tried to get hold of her. My devastation when I couldn't. I spoke about the feeling of helplessness and the grief of losing her when I became Mark Vickers. I spoke about when the chandelier dropped from the ceiling in the hall, our first date at the diner, her picture of the Grand Canyon in our hallway.

I spoke about the clubs we both went to as teenagers, some of them we'd possibly been to at the same time. I told her about bumping into Nikki in Thailand. We'd spoken about Nikki and her infidelity on occasions, usually when I'd had too much to drink. I told her that the Shoelace empire was a complete fallacy created by Juan and the credit card she'd seen me pull a thousand times, had no limit on it.

I told her that I sincerely believed that I had sold my soul, sat on a wall in Spain two years ago to the day.

Jo just sat on my sweater, the sun disappearing over her right shoulder, and listened.

It was an overwhelming amount of information for one person to take on board in such a short space of time, and I just hoped I hadn't gone full overkill and given her some sort of breakdown.

I sat and waited as she continued to run her fingers around the strap of the watch, shoulders rounded, hair hanging limply and tinted red by the sunlight.

I shifted on my backside and pulled my wallet out of my pocket, flicking the credit card towards her. It dropped to the ground by her feet.

I knew she would remember the card. She had asked about the bank it was issued by in a café in LA once when I was paying the bill. She hadn't recognised the name. I'd made a comment about it being only for 'special' people to avoid answering properly, and she'd laughed and said, "…that explains it then." I'd whipped Jo's dessert bowl away from her…"

I'd whipped Jo's dessert bowl away from her and shoved the last mouthful of ice cream into my face before making her watch me devour it with my mouth open. It had earned me a kick in the shins under the table and an apology when it clearly hurt more than it had meant to.

She picked up the credit card and looked at it.

"There is no Banco Deabru," I said. "I looked it up. Deabru means 'evil creature' or 'Demon' or something like that. In some language or another."

Jo raised her head and searched my face frantically with her eyes.

"There're lots about this I don't understand," I continued. "In fact, I don't know how much of this I *do* understand? But I know one thing. I know I love you, and that I have loved you since that first night in that restaurant."

A single tear drew a line down her left cheek.

"I think I felt it. When you fell forward, and I touched your arm?" Jo said, not looking at me but head bowed, fiddling with the watch and the card.

"I know. I saw something in your face."

I wanted to crawl across and take hold of her but wasn't sure if we were quite there yet.

"It's me, Jo. It's Marcus. Well, Mike actually, but apparently it's all relative." I forced a smile as she looked at me and saw the first glimmer of a new expression. Acceptance maybe? I certainly hoped so. Time was running out.

Jo wiped her cheek dry with the sleeve of her sweater and shook her head.

"I'm so sorry you got hurt," I said. "I just didn't know how it was going to play out and when I tried to tell you, they hurt you."

I explained in detail the situation surrounding the broken chandelier and how even thinking about telling her the full story had caused it to crash down and cut to her hand.

"I wanted to call you every one of the three hundred and sixty-four days we've been apart, but I couldn't risk…"

Before I could say anything else, Jo was getting to her feet. Was she going to walk away? Call for help? I froze.

She took two steps forwards and was now standing over me. Still, I couldn't move.

Reaching out with her right hand, I could see the tiny scar from where the glass had cut her.

I took the hand and stood.

She fell into me and quietly sobbed. I bent slightly, completely engulfed her and put her head in my huge hand, unable to stop tears myself.

"It's me, Jo. It's me."

Chapter 16

Jo pushed away from me gently and tried to take all six feet five inches of me, in.

"You're massive!" She laughed through tears that were starting to relent.

"Yeah, took me a bit of getting used to. If you need any jars opening or anything though, you know where to come."

I took both her hands in mine and we stood still for a second in the waning light.

"There're so many things I want to tell you, to talk to you about," I said.

"I'm not sure how much more I can take, to be honest," Jo replied. "I feel like I'm in some bad 'B' movie."

Her face sunk ever so slightly. "What about the 'consequences'? Why haven't they tried to stop you this time and why is that scaring me even more?"

"I honestly don't know. And you're right, it's been playing on my mind since I first saw you stood there."

"Hang on…" said Jo suddenly. "…you said a minute ago 'since you last saw me three hundred and sixty-four days ago'? Are you saying this is your last day as…as you?"

She stepped back; arms stretched out to me '*in this body*'.

I nodded solemnly.

"So how long do we have?" Jo said, her tone one of anger and frustration now.

"It's hard to say. Last time around, I fell asleep on the lawn at some point in the evening and then woke up the next day on the top floor of a hotel in Dubai. I think it's probably any time between now and midnight, but I really am just guessing."

Jo began to pace.

"Give me the watch," she finally said.

I slipped it off my wrist for the second time that evening and handed it to her.

"I've already tried winding it back and getting into the mechanism to change the days. It's a waste of time. I broke two pairs of scissors and your nail file two days before the last change."

Jo ignored me and took the watch before placing it on a small flat rock close by.

She brushed past me and picked up a rock about the size of a cricket ball, examined it, and dropped it again. She scurried around picking up other rocks before dropping them again.

"What are you doing?" I asked her.

"Perfect!" she exclaimed, spotting a basketball-sized rock about ten yards away.

Jo heaved the rock up with both hands and nodded for me to take it from her.

"Maybe it's the watch," she said. "Maybe everything is controlled by the watch. Maybe without the watch, you can't change? It's got to be worth a try? What's the worst that

192

could happen, they've got you by the balls already. Did any of the 'laws' say, 'Don't break the watch'?"

She finished by walking over to the stone with my watch on it and putting her hands on her hips.

"Smash it to fucking pieces." I was shocked by the idea and the fact that I'd never heard her swear.

It felt wrong though. I understood the logic, and she was right, what did I have to lose? I didn't want to 'move on' again without her, regardless of the consequences. But something pulled at my primal instincts. If the watch was the key to all this and had the power to change reality, alter the very fabric of my existence and others around me, smashing it with a rock didn't seem particularly subtle or sensible.

I looked at Jo as I raised the rock above my head. I felt like a chimp about to throw a stone at a nuclear bomb.

"I love you," Jo said. "Do it."

Chapter 17

Darkness

For a moment, I couldn't even tell if my eyes were open or closed.

Or which way up I was. Such was the total disorientation.

I was aware that I was cold.

Blurred light through watery eyes.

Noise.

A familiar noise?

I was laid on my side.

Hard surface.

Shoulder aching.

A breeze chilled my face.

More definition in the light now.

Where's Jo?

Electric lights.

Some moving.

Cars?

A City?

Where's Jo?

Breeze.

Cold.

I'm outside.

I rub my eyes. Squinting. Definitely cars. A bus? Obscured by something. Trees maybe?

A park.

I'm in a park.

Is she here?

"Jo?" I call weakly, my throat dry.

"Come on mate, you know you can't sleep here. Parks closed. Off you trot."

Vision clearing.

Two figures. In hats.

I lift my head.

I know this place. I've been here before.

I'm on a bench.

Uniforms on the figures.

Traffic, trees, buildings. Lots of tall buildings.

Policemen. The older of the two speaking.

"Wakey wakey, pal, let's get going yeah? I've got better things to do than stand around here with you at three in the morning."

I sit myself up and look around.

No sign of Jo.

I do recognise this place.

Hyde Park.

I'm in London.

"That's it, come on, let's go," the older policeman says, grabbing me under the arm and hoicking me up off the bench.

As I get to my feet, I realise I am the shorter of the three men. Certainly not six feet five Mark Vickers anymore.

As I am frogmarched to one of the gates at the north end of the park next to Marble Arch, I rifle through my pockets for my wallet.

Gone.

I shake my wrist subtly and can feel the heavy watch under the layers of a sweater and a thin waterproof jacket that I am wearing. Scruffy jeans and unbranded trainers complete my new outfit.

I touch what feels like a cash note of some denomination in the rear pocket of my jeans and decide not to pull it out until I am away from the Policemen.

The realisation sinks in as I am ushered through a gap in the railings and out onto Park Lane.

"On you go then," I am told by the senior of the two again as they stand and make sure I move away from the park.

I head towards Oxford Street, which is just to my north, for no real reason other than it's where most of the activity seems to be focused.

Once around the corner and out of sight of the fuzz, I slump down against the window of a closed electronic store.

I feel numb. I think there is only so much the human brain can take and it definitely wasn't designed to try and deal with all this.

I reach into my jeans pocket.

One dog eared a fifty-pound note. At least they haven't left me completely destitute I suppose.

Where do I even go from here?

I felt utterly defeated. I'd puffed out my chest, stuck two fingers up to whatever it is controlling all this, and they had stamped on me and crushed me into the dirt like a cockroach.

Despite the hour, people were still busy with their business. Black cabs rumbled up and down Oxford Street, the odd person or group still on the street from a night out in Central London and weary people finishing shifts at bars, hotels, and late-night coffee shops.

I looked at the watch.

'3 6 4'

Jo would still be on top of that Mountain. Thinking about what she must be thinking and feeling now made me feel physically sick.

I patted myself down again. In the inside pocket of the jacket, I could feel a thin piece of plastic. Credit card size and shape. Perhaps I've jumped to conclusions? Perhaps I still have access to all the money?

I pulled the object out.

It wasn't the credit card.

'Blockbuster Video' was emblazoned across the top of the laminated card. Beneath it was what I assumed was my new identity.

'*Mr Matthew Holton*'

Again, I had to applaud their sense of humour. I hadn't returned a copy of 'Trading Places' back in 2010 when Blockbuster went out of business and so officially now probably owed them close to a million pounds in late fees.

I turned to look at my reflection in the window of the shop. I could see a hint of the real me, of Mike Barnes, in the features, only more weathered, older than I remembered.

Mousey brown hair that could have done with a rendezvous with a comb and a couple of days patchy stubble. Not exactly elephant man but I wasn't going to be charming any supermodels onto my park bench any time soon.

Fifty quid and a Blockbuster card. The world was my oyster.

I pulled the hood of the jacket over my head. February in London wasn't quite the same as Dubai or Thailand in terms of temperature.

Something that the monk had said to me popped into my mind '*everything I need and nothing more*'.

Yeah right. I'd rather be licking my wounds on the deck of the yacht, bobbing up and down off the coast of Mauritius with a Margarita, then sat on a chewing gum-poker-dotted pavement in London in a raincoat.

'Do the crime, do the time' I rationalised.

At least I knew what the consequences were now and wondered if Diego had ever broken any of the 'laws' and had to spend a year in similar circumstances. If it was to be just a year? The cloud above my head swelled and grew darker. What if this was it now? What if that was the game? How long can someone like me go before breaking a rule and having to spend the rest of their life like this?

Depression was doing its best to turn to panic.

"It isn't," Juan said sliding his back down the window and sitting next to me on the pavement. He was dressed in a Hawaiian shirt, luminous yellow swimming shorts and boat shoes.

"I wondered when you'd show up," I said, not bothering to look at him and devoid of the energy to do anything else.

"It isn't forever. Not if you stick to the rules this time. You can't have your cake and eat it, Boss!"

"But you bastards put her in front of me! What was I supposed to do?"

"Look, from what I know it was a little test. You just had to let her walk away and wait to change a few hours later. Nobody said this was going to be easy. Although, you should have seen their faces when you tried to smash their watch," Juan grinned and shook his head.

"So what now?" I said.

"Same as before. Clocks ticking. You've got 364 days left as Matt Holton. What you do with that time is yours."

"And if I contact Jo?"

"If you break *any* rules this time, being poor will be the least of your problems," Juan said, standing up and pulling a pair of sunglasses from his head, down onto his face.

"Good luck, boss, as much as I like freezing my balls off here with you, I've got somewhere else to be." He walked away and back around the corner I'd turned a short while before.

"Wait!" I said, jumping to my feet. I had questions that needed answering.

I rounded the corner but the only person within a hundred yards of me on Park Lane was a man shouting at some pigeons next to a bin.

Should have known really. I began to walk.

I ambled West along Oxford Street and eventually South into Bond Street. I passed the high-end jewellery shops from which I could have purchased everything just a matter of hours ago and found myself outside the 'Ritz' Hotel. I was cold in my very core and walking wasn't doing enough to help.

Knowing I only had fifty pounds to my name was preventing me from finding somewhere to sit and have to pay for a coffee but at the stage where I could barely grip the money between my fingers, I decided enough was enough.

I found a twenty-four-hour Turkish café across Green Park and my entire body shuddered with the warmth as I closed the door behind me.

I sat cradling the drink between my hands that tingled as the sensation returned.

Thoughts of Jo washed in and threatened to crush me entirely. To say I was feeling sorry for myself at this stage would be an understatement of historic proportions. I loved Jo more than I had ever loved anything but as I huddled in the corner of that café with forty-six pounds fifty left in my pocket, I decided that I regretted seeing her on the top of that Mountain. I'd given everything I had up, and for what? No boat, no jewellery, no expensive clothes, no cars. Nothing. Just the clothes on my back and fifty quid.

Maybe the Monk could live contentedly with what little resources I have now, or perhaps the Vietnamese farmer could use it to buy a couple of chickens and survive happily for a hundred years, but I wasn't them. I suppose there was the option of passing this so-called gift on to someone else, or at least I assumed there was? But then I'd be stuck as Matthew Bloody Holton? Or be Mike again? I started to feel an intense resentment towards Juan for leaving me with so many unanswered questions.

At the point where my coffee cup had been empty for some time and the café owner was starting to give me a few dirty looks, I got up and stepped back into the bitter February morning.

It was still dark outside, but a milky sun was lazily edging its way to the horizon and there was a hint of light playing at the roofs of the buildings. The streets were far busier now as the Capital City was starting to wake and people unlucky enough to have the early shifts were making their way to their jobs.

I spent the day trudging the streets of Central London, my mind wandering between thoughts of Jo and thoughts of Juan and the possibility of him appearing at any moment and bundling me into a Limo 'only joking!' he'd say in my fantasy, and whisk me off to the Dorchester or the Savoy. But he never came. I realised after a few hours that the unpleasant aroma of the City in my nostrils was actually me.

Quelling the sense of panic became the biggest challenge.

I turned corner after iconic corner. I was a sullen and depressive tourist outside the Houses of Parliament, The Shard, The London Eye and Buckingham Palace. I knew I needed to use the little money I had sparingly and at sunset counted thirty-two pounds eighty and a stomach far from satisfied.

What followed was the worst night of my life. I had arrived too late at a homeless shelter I'd read about in a discarded 'Metro' and was naive without a plan 'b'. It was simply too cold to lay on the pavement, even the homeless people, *other* homeless people, had blankets or cardboard to at least help against the freezing temperatures.

How did they do this every night? If I managed to make it through a year as Matt Holton, I swore I would never walk past someone sleeping rough again without giving them everything I had in my pockets.

I dragged myself around, freezing and bleary-eyed, from all-night coffee shops to 24-hour McDonalds, to Bagel shops, desperately trying to spend as little money as possible and catch a moment's sleep before being spotted and moved on.

By sun up next day, I was exhausted.

I was awoken from a two-minute sleep on my own arm in a café just after six a.m. by the sound of the bell above the door ringing as a customer entered.

It was a young guy, white but with dreadlocks and a guitar case slung over his back. He ordered some sort of sandwich and a tea to take away and exchanged a few words with the girl behind the counter. There was a familiarity that made me think this was part of both of their daily routines.

"Where are you today?" the girl said.

"Baker Street station. Can't grumble, did alright there last time, although I did pull an expired condom and an opal fruit out at the end of the day too. Might try a couple of new ones I've been playing with, reckon if I do 'Hotel California' once more I might go mental."

He was obviously about to start a day busking. A day picking up change from commuters, entertaining them for those few moments as they hurried past.

I could do that.

Not only had I spent a fortune on guitar lessons, but I'd spent most evenings on the Yacht and then whilst travelling Vietnam and Thailand, playing alone or, after suitable lubrication, to a few travelling companions. I was genuinely pretty good by the time I hit South America and had learned to bang out enough tunes I could fit my limited singing range around.

I counted my money again. Twenty-one pounds fifteen pence.

I'd bought five guitars during my time as Marcus and then Mark, the most expensive being one owned by Elvis Presley that I paid just over a million dollars for, played 'Wonderwall' on once and then hung on the wall in one of my downstairs bathrooms, and the cheapest a two-thousand-dollar Fender.

I moved the coins around the sticky table as if that would somehow magically make them multiply.

"Excuse me mate!" I said to the Busker as he turned to leave the café. "I wonder if you could help me?"

I grilled him about how busking worked, what I needed to look out for, where I could and couldn't potentially set up and where the best pitches were. He couldn't have been more helpful, and I got the sense that it was a bit of a community. I gave him a pound to start his day of tips off, despite this leaving me just twenty pounds now.

It was just the twinkling of a plan starting to take shape in my mind.

I had to force thoughts of Jo and James and Monks and Diego and Yachts and watches and everything else from the past two years from my mind. *This* was my reality for the next 363 days.

The girl behind the counter seemed friendly enough, and at a quiet moment, I asked if she wouldn't mind googling on her phone for music shops and second-hand shops. I scribbled down the addresses and phone numbers of the half dozen she managed to find within a few miles and thanked her before heading off to the first one, realising I couldn't afford to use what previous little money I had left on making lots of potentially wasted phone calls.

The first on the route I had vaguely planned, took me to a music shop where the cheapest guitar was almost two-hundred pounds. The second was a 'Cash Converter' that had an electric guitar, still too expensive even if I had an amp and power and everything else I would need to play it.

I walked into the third, my enthusiasm starting to wain and anxiety starting to tug at my consciousness again. I still had to find a guitar for under twenty pounds, get a bit of practice in and find a spot somewhere before making enough money to pay for a room tonight.

However, leaning against the far wall of the second-hand shop, amongst some old golf clubs and a couple of wooden tennis rackets, was a shabby looking acoustic guitar. I nodded to the guy in the shop who returned a friendly smile before going back to scratching his head and flicking through some paperwork on the counter.

I picked up the guitar. It had all six strings that was a good sign and looked like it may have been a decent piece of equipment when it was made, possibly upwards of twenty years ago.

A small tag on a piece of string hung from one of the tuning keys.

'£40'.

"Hiya," I said to the guy pouring through a mound of invoices on his desk. "I am interested in the guitar?"

The man peered over the top of some half-rimmed glasses and squinted in the direction of the guitar.

"Forty pounds mate. It's a good one. Quality. Just needs a bit of TLC and it will be around long after we are!" He chortled to himself, clearly pleased with his pitch.

"Yeah, I'm sure," I said. "The thing is though, I only have twenty pounds?"

The man didn't look up this time.

"I've got a painting of a guitar I can do you for that?" he said, tapping away on an ancient-looking calculator.

"Yeah, erm, I really need a guitar to be honest though."

"Sorry, pal, 'no can do' I paid more than that for it myself."

The guitar looked as if it had been stood there for years and so I persisted, emptying my pockets onto the counter.

"This really is everything I have, and I'm pretty desperate. *Really* desperate actually."

"Look, what can I say? I'm trying to run a business here, it's hard enough nowadays as it is. Sorry mate." To be fair, the man looked genuinely guilty that he wasn't able to help, and I understood his position.

I scraped the notes and remaining coins from the counter and shovelled them back into my pocket.

"Thanks anyway," I said and slumped despondently to the exit pulling the crumpled paper with addresses scribbled on it from my pocket.

"Wait a sec," the man said with a sigh as I grasped the door handle. "I tell you what. I have a van full of old crap out the back that needs unloading into the storeroom. If you can do that for me, you can have the guitar for twenty quid. What do you say?"

"Yes!" I replied excitedly "Absolutely! Just point me in the right direction!"

We shook hands, me more enthusiastically than him, and I followed him through the store, past an unhygienic looking toilet and through a room that was filled to the rafters with all sorts of tat from lampshades to suitcases to an orthopaedic bed.

It was a large box van and was indeed 'full of old crap' as he had promised.

It took me well over two hours to finally get everything off and into the storeroom. I was exhausted, and when I eventually finished and flopped down onto an old armchair at the back of the shop, the owner appeared with a steaming cup of tea and a plate of Jaffa cakes, which I gratefully inhaled.

"Here you go," He said handing me the guitar, as I slurped down the last of the tea.

"Thanks," I said, pulling the last of my funds from my pocket.

"Don't worry about it," the man said, shaking his head and stepping away from me "Just nice for someone to get some use out of the old thing. Don't forget me if you turn out to be the next Ed Sheeran though, OK?"

Not only did I now have the instrument I needed but I had a head start on my 'bed for the night' fund.

"Thank you," I said. Some of my faith in humanity was restored.

We shook hands again as I left with the guitar slung over my back on the threadbare strap.

Logic told me to go somewhere that people had plenty of disposable income to lavish on a hard-working and impoverished musician.

I returned to the 'Ritz' hotel and found a spot on the covered section outside that looked ideal. As I went to pull the guitar off my back, however, I realised I had absolutely nothing to use to collect the 'donations'. I walked over to a litter bin and had to carefully select the cleanest paper coffee cup to use until I could find something more suitable and less disgusting.

I hadn't even placed the cup on the ground before the doorman wandered calmly over to me and with a warm and jovial smile, told me to 'fuck off'.

I made my way back to Green Park, remembering a spot that would provide me with some cover from the elements but plenty of people walking past to potentially extract money from.

It was tough.

By the end of the first day I'd played my repertoire of twelve songs so many times I wanted to set fire to my guitar for warmth.

Sixteen pounds thirty-seven.

My fingers hurt so bad I wanted to cry.

By the time I'd bought a sandwich from a Tesco Local, I only had enough money for a room for the night in a place that smelled of cabbage and cheese and even then, I'd need to make more money to be able to buy breakfast.

It was hard not to lay in bed that night and think about everything I had just a day or so ago or what it would be like, even in the cabbage/cheese room, to have Jo here next to me.

Twelve months.

I wasn't going to give whoever or whatever it was messing with me, the satisfaction of seeing me giving up.

The next few days gradually got easier. It became unseasonably warm which not only made the day less painful, but more people were out and about and more willing to stop for a few seconds and put their hand in their pocket.

As I started to learn the best places, the songs that got people chucking in coins and my own confidence built, the revenue increased. Some days I even had two meals. I'd spend the evenings learning new songs and soon increased my songbook significantly.

About two weeks in, and after a particularly profitable day in which a Japanese tourist clearly threw the wrong note into my cup, I treated myself to a pint at a pub round the corner from the room I was staying in.

It was a Friday night and heaving. The bar was four deep and the landlord was running up and down like a mad man to try and get everyone served. The crowd was growing restless and some people even began to leave.

Brian, behind the bar, was repeatedly apologising and explaining that neither of his staff had turned up for work. I took my days takings out of my pocket and looked at it. Enough for another pint, tonight's room and a sausage and egg McMuffin.

I made my way to the serving hatch at the end of the bar.

"Excuse me?" I tried to shout above the noise. "Excuse me! Do you want a hand?"

"Eh?" Brian shouted whilst pouring a pint of Heineken with one hand and grabbing a packet of prawn cocktail crisps with the other.

"Want me to help out for a bit? I've worked bars before, just 'til you get on top of this lot?"

Brian looked dubious but as he dropped a handful of change onto the floor and it rolled around his feet he looked well and truly beaten.

"Yeah. Sure. Crack on," he said eyeing me up suspiciously, and me making the most inoffensive face I could.

"Tenner an hour. Cash. That OK?" I said, taking off my jacket and throwing it onto a stool behind the bar.

"Eight," Brian shouted back while drawing some whisky from one of the optics.

"Done!" I shouted back. "Yes, mate, what can I get you?"

We both quickly realised that me not knowing how to use a card machine or the computerised till was almost making the whole process slower, however, after twenty minutes or so of fumbling through, we found a system of me serving the drinks and Brian predominantly taking payment and helping punters in between.

I loved every second of it. It had been a lonely couple of weeks and the banter with the customers and vibrancy of the place was a real tonic. I was disappointed when Brian rung 'last orders.

"Any chance you're around tomorrow night?" Brian said as he pushed the final bolt into place on the front door around midnight.

I was sat, tired but content on a stool at the bar, a pint of San Miguel in front of me courtesy of the last group to leave who had won some money at the greyhounds that evening.

"Look Brian, I'm 'between jobs' at the minute, I'll take whatever shifts you have."

"It's the third time Sandra's let me down this week. I'm getting shot. Jobs yours if you want it, you pull a decent pint and the punters seem to like you. You might want to tone down some of the stories though, make them a bit more believable in future."

I thought about it for all of ten seconds. I could busk between shifts, keep my eye in, and work at the pub the rest of the time. I might even be able to rustle enough money together to rent a proper room at some point.

Life became bearable, and I found myself looking at the counter on my watch less and less. I missed Jo and the Yacht and some of the friends I'd met in Asia and Captain Toni, but the end of every day I got through felt like '*sticking it to the man*'.

Perhaps living in one room and working in a pub *was* more bearable knowing that it had a definitive end that I'd marked on the calendar from the Chinese restaurant in my room, but I hadn't had that amount of genuine interaction with people for a long time. The job I quit before moving to Spain was based at a desk in my own cubicle where I might talk to three people in a day. Even in Vegas, and travelling East after that, I would spend swathes of time on my own, reading, playing the guitar, or knocking five irons off the back of the boat on my own.

I got to know the regulars, and although the weekends were busy, I looked forward to the atmosphere and buzz of the place.

Particularly Saturdays.

Brian always had a live band in the pub on a Saturday. I would listen to song arrangements and set lists and steel ideas for my busking that I kept up even when working almost full time at the pub.

One particular Saturday evening, I had been at the pub for about six months and was even opening up for Brian at times, I was serving one of the regulars when I became aware of raised voices coming from where that evening's band were setting up. There seemed to be some sort of 'artistic differences' in regard to whether or not they should finish their set with 'Mr Brightside' or not.

"But we always close with that Tom!" A scruffy-looking guy tuning a bass guitar said despairingly.

"Exactly! It's such a fucking cliché! Why don't we try and do something a bit different!" another guy was saying whilst unclipping the catches on his guitar case.

"Coz that's what people want to bloody hear Rob, that's why," a chap tightening bolts on a high-hat next to a drum kit said, clearly bored of a conversation it sounds like they'd had on more than one occasion.

This continued throughout me changing the channel on the TV and unloading glasses from the dishwasher.

The argument raged on.

"Fine!" Guitar case guy suddenly said, "I fucking well will!" and with that, he grabbed his guitar, pushed past the drummer who was by now doing the job of separating the other two members of his band, and stormed from the pub.

"Sorry, Brian," one of them shouted. "Rob's being a dick again. If we can't get him back, then we won't be able to play tonight mate."

"This is the last time fellas. I have people coming here expecting live music, if you can't give it to them then I can't keep booking you."

I recognised them as a band I'd seen play in the pub a month or so before. Usual covers, a bit of Oasis, a bit of Beetles, a bit of Ed Sheeran. Nothing particularly groundbreaking. Nothing I couldn't bumble my way through.

"I might be able to help out," I chirped up. "I play a bit, have you got the playlist there?"

"What do you mean 'a bit'? It's not amateur hour mate, we are professionals." The scruffy Bass player said.

"Shut up Colin you knobhead," the drummer said, handing me the list of songs from tonight's gig. "What do you play?"

I read through the list.

"Some of these I won't have a problem with, but I might need the chords for a few others. How long have we got?" I said slipping behind the bar and grabbing my guitar which I had from the morning busking at New Bond Street.

The two remaining members of the band huddled together, looking over their shoulders at me occasionally before breaking and turning to me.

"Why not, let's do this."

Brian had to be placated by me agreeing to do an extra shift next week as he was now short-staffed but equally glad not to have to explain to a bunch of angry drinkers where their live music was.

I am not going to say it was seamless, far from it, but it was still one of the best nights of my life. I'd never played in a band before and most people had only ever heard me play four bars of 'Summer of 69' on their way to work. It was possibly the most alive I'd ever felt and at the end of the gig, Colin, the Bass Guitarist, handed me seventy-five quid.

When the regular guitarist didn't show up for the next practice, I got a call from the drummer asking if I'd be interested in jamming with them one afternoon and seeing how it goes. I said 'YES!' and before long I was having to book shifts off from the pub to play gigs at other local venues. I was meeting all sorts of people, playing to crowds of eight people one night but a hundred on another, depending on the size of the pub or club.

I would ask myself why I had never done anything like this before? I could have had guitar lessons when I was working in the office or when I met Nikki? Wanting to run away to Spain was really running away from the mundanity of everyday life. Maybe I just never looked around at what I could have gotten out of it if I'd given it any thought. If I'd put any effort in. I was just surviving before, not *living*.

I was never short of people to have a chat or pint with and there were also plenty of opportunities for 'romantic rendezvous' especially as the guitarist in a band at a wedding. Apparently, bridesmaids love a musician. But I knew I'd find Jo one day. I could feel it.

Next time I saw Juan, I wasn't going to let him leave without answering my questions or telling me what I needed to do to be with Jo. Still, I suspected that I might have to make a choice between keeping the wealth or going back to a normal life if I wanted to be with her. If I was given a choice at all.

It had occurred to me that I could still be a trillionaire and be in a band and have friends. Even work in a pub. Work in a pub and live on a Super Yacht. I felt like one of those lottery winners who win the euro millions and keeps their job in Morrisons.

The watch ticked on.

Choices would have to be made.

Chapter 18

My third Christmas since meeting Diego approached. I was starting to get used to the speed with which those last couple of months would pass by. The nervous excitement of what would come next, increased this time as I had a list of questions for Juan ready for when I transitioned again. I knew I only had a year, but I decided not to avoid making connections with people next time, to be committed to situations, live in the moment, come what may.

I'd found that the more I invested in other people's problems, challenges, realities, the more invested I felt in my own. I couldn't spend eternity travelling the world, a lone wolf pining after the woman I'd lost or dealt with the consequences of finding her.

The best times I'd had since that bar in Spain were times I'd shared with other people and rarely as a direct result of the money.

Don't get me wrong, some of the Vegas parties were incredible, but if I could go back and relive any of the last few years (other than just watching Netflix with Jo) it would have been some of the nights spent in Vietnam with friends, a six-pack of cheap local beer and banging out some golden oldies on the guitar. Or even some of the nights on stage with the band maybe.

I'd told Brian and the band at a very early stage that I was going travelling not too far into the New Year, and I wouldn't be around forever. Both tried to persuade me to put this off, and I would humour them occasionally. However, I'd decided months ago that I wanted to head back to Sri Lanka for the last couple of weeks as Matt Holton.

I wanted to find that Monastery again and speak to the old Monk. He seemed to know things, and if this was the life I was now going to be living, of choices and changes, potentially solitude, I wanted his counsel, some guidance from him. I wanted to know what he knew.

Christmas week was mayhem at the pub, on top of which we had gigs booked right through to New Year and beyond. This was all working out perfectly as I was squirrelling the extra money away for my one-way ticket to Sri Lanka.

January came and went, and I'd been patient with finding and booking a ticket that would still take almost every penny I'd managed to save. I eventually found a flight that would work and was within budget.

I made the most of the last few performances with the band and the last few shifts at the pub. The last of each, equally emotional. I cried like a baby as our lead singer crooned his way through 'Leaving on a Jet Plane' at my last wedding.

The previous eleven and a half months had been a greater journey for me than sailing halfway around the world, despite the entire thing taking place within a few square miles of London. From being kicked out of coffee shops, asleep on the table, hurting and alone, to being part of something bigger than me, something that filled me up, something real. The greatest joys from that year weren't just seeing a crowd bouncing up and down at somebody's fortieth or being propositioned by, occasionally, attractive women after a set, but sometimes just in a conversation with a regular in the pub and hearing their story.

Don't get me wrong, if I need to get from A to B, I'd rather do it in a Lamborghini than my Fiat, but not being able to fill my time with expensive distractions taught me a thing or two about finding contentment in every day. That Dalai Lama knew what he was talking about you know.

I had a few ideas about what I would do with my next twelve months.

If only there was some way I could get Jo back, and she could be part of it with me.

Let's see what my Monk friend had to say about it all.

Chapter 19

The last time I'd arrived in Sri Lanka it had been via the Indian Ocean, and on a luxury Yacht designed specifically for the comfort and pleasure of its passengers.

This time, I'd flown Turkish Air economy on a sixteen-hour flight with two stops, next to a woman with foot fungus.

Columbo airport was bedlam. Tourists, businessmen, backpackers, families crying hellos and goodbyes, soldiers, salesmen and security staff.

I managed to navigate my way through the arrivals lounge and out into the humidity of the day. The shock following a British Winter, and overzealous aircon setting on the plane meant the heat hit me in the chest like a brick.

I loved my time in Sri Lanka last time and so arrived there with over two weeks to go and time to absorb as much of the place as I could. I had the name of some cheap places I could stay and my route deep into the countryside via a complex pattern of bus routes all scribbled down and ready to put to the test.

It had been a gruelling flight and within five minutes of being huddled up next to my backpack on the dilapidated bus that would begin my two-day journey into the mountains, I started to drift off. Despite what had been twelve important and humbling months of personal growth and discovery, as we bounced along the potholed roads and sleep became irresistible, I did start to fantasise about all the comforts that would soon be accessible to me again. I loved the banter of the pub and the adrenalin of playing in a packed hall for a wedding or birthday but I also loved sleeping in beds big enough to park your car in and garages big enough to park a house in.

I slipped into slumber and dreamt that I was at a five-star resort by the pool with Jo. Could have been the Bahamas, Hawaii, Seychelles, who knows. I was sipping some sort of cocktail that in my dream was the size of a washing up bowl when I realised Jo was flailing around in the pool, drowning. I couldn't seem to get off my sunbed quickly enough, my legs simply not doing what I wanted them to do.

At the point, I realised I wasn't going to make it to her in time, and she disappeared below the surface of the water, I woke with a jump. Trees whipped by outside my window as I tried to slow my heart rate and kill some more time by falling back to sleep. We wouldn't reach the next stop until nightfall.

I spent the next week trying to stay as 'off-grid' as possible. Overconfidence became an issue as the last time I'd been in Sri Lanka it had been with a guide, bought and paid for, who smoothed the path in front of me whilst still managing to make me feel like Bear Grylls.

Suddenly, thrust into a country where I didn't speak the language and that had an infrastructure that made my sock draw look organised, I realised I was out of my depth. I spent one night under a tree during which I became a meal for every insect in South East Asia and another on a bench at a bus station.

I reached the edge of the village above which the monastery sat, with *'0 0 6'* showing on the watch.

It felt like the end of an epic quest or long dreamt of pilgrimage. Extra shifts and skipping meals had funded me being here now, as well as enduring other people's foot fungus, sharing a bus seat with a chicken for eight hours and spending the last three days scratching every inch of my sunburned and bitten skin.

I reached the last step at the top of the hill both weary and elated.

Of course, I worried that the old monk might not be there, I didn't know how 'Monking' worked? For all, I knew they got seconded to other monasteries or disappeared into the forests for months on end to meditate about leaves. It did also occur to me that it had been well over a year since my last visit and the old man was frail and apparently over a hundred years old then. It would be just my luck if he had selfishly gone and died last week.

I needn't have worried.

There he was, sat, legs crossed on the same tattered mat, dextrously weaving one leaf over another into baskets. A pile of six or seven completed baskets threatened to topple over behind him and a pile of leaves next to him looked like another six or seven would be added before sunset.

"Hello again," he said without looking up from his work. "I didn't expect to see you back so soon." A smile crept across his lined face.

"When you came here the first time, I had been expecting someone else. A nice man, a Spanish man if I recall correctly. I am guessing you have met this man too?"

"Yes, I have. His name was Diego. He's the one that tricked me into this."

"You seem angry with him?" the old man said sounding surprised. "If you had known the terms in more detail, would you have declined his offer? Would you have walked away and continued as you were?"

The monk continued to fold leaf over leaf as he spoke to me, only occasionally looking up from his work.

Since losing Jo the first time, I had cursed Diego and the vagueness with which he described what would happen. I resented how he had manipulated me into shaking his hand and taking the heavy burden of this life from him. I'd never considered what I would have done given the freedom of making a more informed decision. But the answer was obvious.

Of course, I would have gladly shaken his hand. An orphan pool cleaner with a failed marriage, a mild drink problem and absolutely no prospects for improving any of that? How could I possibly have said no? I couldn't have known I'd find everything I wanted in that first year, everything I needed to be truly happy. Perhaps Diego had never found it. Or worse, perhaps he had.

I watched clouds roll across the incomprehensibly vast sky joined by billows of smoke from the village below as meals were cooked in the tiny wooden houses.

The pile of leaves next to the old man was slowly shrinking and being replaced by a growing stack of baskets behind him.

"How do you know about me, and Diego and the deal we both made?"

I finally said, "And do you know of any way I can be with someone, properly, someone I love? It seems that not being able is simply the cruellest punishment, but I don't know what I'm being punished for? I wasn't perfect, I was lazy at work I suppose, wasn't a great husband, and I could have done more to help other people I suppose, but hey, me and the rest of the world, right?"

The old man placed a half-completed basket on the mat in front of him and folded his fingers together. He didn't speak but simply sat in thought. After a short while, he looked at me with sympathetic eyes.

"Every adversity is a welcome lesson that we should embrace and rejoice in, do you not think? I have lived a long life, suffering is part of life, but suffering brings us perspective, allows us to recognise the times of joy.

"Are you being punished, or have you been given a gift to cherish? Ask yourself what you have learned in your time with the many faces. That you are here, sat with me now, tells me that you may have learned what's truly important, so quickly into your journey too. It took me far longer."

Something in his face, in his expression as he finished talking and looked at me.

"You don't mean it took you *'far longer'* in the context of a normal person's life, do you?"

The old man's gaze didn't faulter from mine.

"Who are you? Really?" I asked.

"He was once the same as you," came a voice from behind me. A soft Spanish accent.

I turned.

Diego.

I should have been more surprised to see him stood there on the steps of the monastery, but by this stage, I probably could have seen Celine Dion singing 'My heart will go on' on the roof and barely raised an eyebrow.

"The same as *us* you mean, surely?"

Diego was stood with the same perfectly coiffured hair and expensive-looking clobber as the night I'd met him at Churchill's. He looked 'lighter'. Not in terms of his weight, but less intense in some way, less sad, less anxious, a heavy burden removed from his shoulders maybe.

"No," Diego said. "Not the same as *us.*"

I heard a door close somewhere nearby and footsteps on the wooden platform that formed the perimeter of the Monastery. These footsteps grew louder until a figure dressed in the traditional orange Monk's cassock rounded the corner. Even in unfamiliar clothing and sporting a shaved head, there was no mistaking who it was.

"What do you think eh, Boss?" Juan said, twirling on his sandals, arms spread and inviting me to critique his outfit.

It was all I could do to shake my head at Juan as I slumped down onto a step and before gravity and my spinning head, got the better of me. I closed my eyes and concentrated on my breathing. It was all a bit much quite frankly.

I was aware of the rustling of the leaves as the Monk entwined one with another and felt Diego sit down to my left and Juan to my right. Three brass monkeys sat on top of the world, the Sri Lankan countryside sprawled far below us.

Nobody spoke, I knew they were giving me time to find some sort of foundation in reality again.

"OK," I finally said. "I give up. What the fucking fuck is fucking happening?"

I looked first at Juan, then turned to Diego. The Monk simply continued weaving his little baskets. The urge to go and kick his pile down the mountain was building uncontrollably.

Juan sighed. "So it's like this, Boss," he said pointing to the Monk. "Our friend here, well, is Barry."

"*Barry?*" I replied doubtfully.

"Barry," Juan said. "He has been on a similar journey to you. As you kinda guessed. He found this place and decided he wanted to stay. So we let him."

"You let him?"

"We let him."

"Why didn't I get given a choice?" I squealed, emotions balanced somewhere between tears and extreme violence.

"You weren't ready. You're a baby in terms of how this normally goes. You're my biggest professional achievement! Barry did almost thirty years before he found his 'Happy Place'."

"His *Happy Place*?" I asked.

"His 'Happy Place'," Juan repeated. "But you found your true soul mate! Rarely happens. We had an idea there was good compatibility when we chucked you two together but nobody realised we'd found a stage five soul mate match."

"A stage five soul mate match?" I shrugged my shoulders in defeat, the conversation so beyond me I didn't really know why I was bothering to ask.

"Yeah," Juan continued. "Look, make yourself comfortable, I'm gonna tell you a little story…"

As I sat and listened, as the Monk (or Barry) sat and made his baskets and Diego nodded along, Juan explained in as simple terms as possible, how and why everything that had happened, had happened.

He explained that he was known as a 'Fixer'. That Diego was another 'Fixer' in his 'department' and for all intents and purposes, they shared a desk and helped each other out with assignments. I didn't bother questioning any of this.

Their job was to 'make things right' when someone upstairs had, for want of a better expression, fucked up. They would ensure that people 'got the happiness they should have had' and 'got what they deserved' if the fuck up hadn't have happened.

Juan explained that Diego hadn't had 'The Gift' and was simply playing a character they'd created whilst chatting next to the coffee machine one day in the office. He was embarrassed by the title but when pushed described himself and Diego as 'kind of Guardian Angels but less poncey' as apparently, and I quote 'they are all a bunch of goody-goody wankers'.

Juan did the shaking, balled fist, gesture, to emphasise this. Diego's story was largely true but had happened to another person who had been 'fixed' and apparently it fitted with my situation and circumstances at the time and saved them the effort of coming up with something original.

Juan stopped and paused for a second, and I saw him glance briefly at Diego, his face suddenly more solemn.

"Mike," he continued. "That day your mum fell under the train? Someone took their eye off the ball upstairs. It won't make you feel any better to hear all the details but, cutting a long story short, there was a mix up with a fag break and, well, nobody was watching as things developed down on Platform 4 that day. Your mum, your beautiful, caring, sweet, funny mum, wasn't supposed to pass over on that Tuesday.

"The guy with the stolen purse was supposed to trip and have a life-changing, near-death experience that made him alter the course of his life. He was supposed to go on and help ex-cons make something of their lives.

"None of that happened and your mum, well, your mum was the truly awful, collateral damage."

There are no words for the feelings that hearing something like that floods you with.

She had been my rock, my teacher, my role model. She had been my best friend.

To hear that she was never supposed to die, that I'd lost a lifetime of potential memories we should have shared, through someone not doing their job properly, was all far, far, too much. I put my head in my hands, cried like a baby and was even grateful for Juan's arm around my shoulders.

As I started to regain some sort of composure, and whilst wiping snot from my face, I had questions.

"So how has any of this, 'fixed' anything?"

Diego spoke this time, "With such a colossal 'mistake', there's a lot to unravel, to change, to fix. You won't have noticed at the time but the people you met on your journey since that night we met in Roquetas, all gave you something you would have got from your Mother had you had that time with her. Captain Toni, Rosh your guide, Mr Nguyen the farmer, Jo, all gave you something you will have absorbed without knowing."

Juan took over.

226

"And it allows us to watch you, to observe and see what you need. These extreme situations are the best way to find out what we can do for you so that the next 'phase' of your life, in some ways makes up, even if just a bit, for the first part. Does that make sense?"

I suppose it did. Sort of.

"Why did it take you so long to step in and help me out then? My teens were bloody miserable and then I met Nikki, and look how that turned out."

"We like to see if you can sort yourself out if things 'fix' themselves," said Juan. "Sometimes they do and it's always preferable. Like letting a chick fight its way through its shell? We hoped Nikki might get you back on track. Sorry about that. When things went south the way they did, we realised it was time to take action."

I was speaking because it seemed the appropriate thing to do at the time but the whole thing was so dream-like that if I'd woken up in bed next to Nikki suddenly then I wouldn't have been remotely surprised.

"So I haven't sold my soul? You aren't minions of the Devil, sent to torment me for eternity?" I asked, turning my head both ways, not sure who to ask the question of.

"Far from it, Boss," Juan said smiling.

That was a relief I suppose. Wouldn't have been ideal.

"And what about making me sleep on a park bench, the agony of losing Jo? How the hell did any of that help me? What about my next 'change'? How will all that work?"

"It's all taken care of, Boss. You have nothing to worry about, I promise. There won't be any more fuck-ups upstairs. You are kind of like a VIP client now! You needed to have the bad times to appreciate the good. Nobody truly knows themselves until they have experienced the best and the worst they can handle. You now know what that means for you. We just find it works out better in the long run."

"I get that I've learned about the true value of things and that money can't buy happiness blah, blah, blah, congratulations, but when I left England, I was living in a smelly bedsit in Green Park. Not sure I fancy going back to that regardless of how 'enlightened' I might be. I'm not bloody Barry I'm afraid."

"If your Mum had been alive, you'd have gone on to achieve things, Mike. She'd have supported you and guided you and you'd have reached your full potential. That would have come with a certain level of financial reward that you never got. We'll rebalance that, don't you worry."

The Monk stood, straightened his pile of baskets and looked straight at me.

"You will always have questions. I still have them now. And life is rarely fair, I've learned that. But accept this gift for what it is. None of it will bring your Mother back, it didn't bring my Wife back, but it certainly helped with the life with which I was left."

With that, he shuffled across the wooden veranda, turned, bowed his head to Juan and Diego, and disappeared around a corner.

Diego now stood also.

"It was good to see you again my friend," he said holding out his hand for me to shake. I was extremely reluctant after the last time I'd shaken that hand but something in his face told me there was nothing to worry about. He smiled at me, clearly realising my dilemma. I bit the bullet and shook his hand. An enthusiastic shake before he nodded at Juan, gave me one more smile and set off down the mountainside through the archway of leaves and branches.

"So what now?" I said, just me and Juan sat next to each other on the wooden step, now in the shadow of the Temple behind us, the sun beginning to drop below the peak of the Mountain.

"Go where you need to go to be happy, Boss. If that's back on the yacht, just say the word. If that's the Penthouse Suite at the Palazzo, you're there. No problem. Your call."

"Will I see you again Juan? Will I open up my wardrobe door one day and you'll jump out and help yourself to my best Whisky?"

"Nope, you don't have to worry about that anymore. I'll check in on you now and again from up there, but there'll be nobody stealing your booze."

Despite what a pain in my arse he'd been, the thought made me feel sad.

"Thanks for everything," I said holding my hand out to Juan. He looked dubious and furrowed his brow nervously. "I mean it," I said, before he pushed my arm aside and grabbed me up in a bear hug, squeezing the air from my lungs and leaving me with bruised ribs.

"Sorry…" Juan mumbled. "Now, haven't you got somewhere to be, Boss?"

Chapter 20

"Matt!" shouted Ross, our Bass guitarist, as I stepped through the door of 'The George' huddled up in my coat, my protection against a typically cold February evening in London.

"What are you doing back? Thought you'd be sunning yourself in Oz or California by now? Run out of money already?" he chuckled.

"Something like that," I smiled back across the busy pub. Live music Friday.

The rest of the band looked up from tuning their instruments or supping their pints, up on the small stage at the back of the pub. One or two punters looked up to see what all the shouting was about.

Sat at a small sticky table, deeply engrossed in conversation with a friend, was the most beautiful woman I had ever seen. Slim, with long dark hair, a few strands of which had fallen from a ponytail and were trailing across her face. As I approached, she pushed the hair behind her ear.

I'd rehearsed what I was going to say a million times but words, as they always seemed to at these times, failed me. I found myself standing awkwardly close to the table at which she was sitting, forced towards it by how packed the pub was. The woman and her friend suddenly found themselves sitting in my shadow, causing them to stop talking and look up at me with something between concern and annoyance.

"Hi, Jo," I managed to say. "I'm Matt. I mean Mark. My name is Mark. But I think you know that."

The woman's expression changed from annoyance to realisation and as she brought her hand to her mouth a tear dropped from her left eye and splashed down onto a 'Fosters' beer mat.

Chapter 21

"I'm sure this is it, but it's been six years, it's hard to say. That'll do. Stop here please mate!"

This wasn't the first time I'd found myself on this dirt track in a car that was barely roadworthy.

I paid the driver and we stood and watched him turn in the road and head back to town. I looked about, the countryside doing its level best to overwhelm me as it always did in this part of the world. Bamboo, Palm and Mangroves fought for light in the shade of the Mountainous terrain.

"Have I told you how long we wandered around these fields for? I was bloody starving, started imagining my mate Pete as a giant walking, talking Roast Chicken. Thought we might die out here."

"You're soooo dramatic," Jo grumbled. "And yes, you have told me. A few times. Now hold James, I've been bouncing him up and down for the last twenty-five miles while you gawped at the trees like an idiot."

Jo handed me our son, who had apparently decided to save his travel sickness for my shoulder and swiftly threw up all down my back. Failing to suppress a giggle, Jo scrambled in one of the bags for something to clean me up with.

I was confident our destination lay at the end of what you could have called a driveway but was really just a mud strip where the trees were far enough apart to drive a small vehicle through. After fifty yards or so we turned a tight bend and a small house edged into view. I could see rusted, ancient farm tools strewn throughout the scene and hear chickens clucking in their coop. Parked in the shade of a tired old Palm was the Citroen C5.

An elderly Vietnamese woman was stooped over the chickens scattering feed and her husband was pulling sticks of bamboo into bundles. Neither of them saw my family and me as we approached. They wouldn't have recognised me if they had.

"Mr Nguyen?" I called, swapping James from one arm to the other.

The old man turned, as did his wife, and dropping his bundle strode towards us. His sure-footedness belying his age. He said something I didn't understand but by the look on his face assumed it was something along the lines of 'who the bloody hell are you lot and what do you want'.

As he got closer, he smiled and twisted to see James who was fighting me to turn around and see what was going on.

"Mr Nguyen, sorry to intrude, and I realise you probably have no idea what I'm saying," I blabbered while Jo shook her head and smiled, motioning for me to hand her back our fidgety offspring.

"But a friend of mine made a promise to you some years back. A promise to pay you back for some kindness and generosity you showed to him and his friend. He couldn't pay you at the time but swore he'd pay you back someday. He can't be here I'm afraid, but I said I'd fulfil that promise for him. He said the kindness you showed changed how he looked at the world."

I pulled some cash from my pocket and gestured towards the car whilst making charades like steering movements. I also made an eating gesture with my hands to represent us eating his food all those years ago. I could sense Jo stifling a full-on laugh at my rubbish mimes.

The old man clearly had no idea what the hell I was going on about, and I continued to try and explain as his wife spotted baby James, now fascinated by the manic chickens. With a beaming smile, she motioned for Jo and Juan to follow her over for a closer look.

I was trying to tell my story again whilst interspersing it with as much French and hand gestures as I was able when the old man cut me off with a friendly wave of his hand. He moved aside and invited me to take a seat next to a pot of simmering food. It looked like I'd be eating with them again, and they likely wouldn't take 'no' for an answer. James was cooing over by the stupid birds and Jo looked over her shoulder at me with a proud smile, pushing some hair behind her ear with her free hand. I got a whiff of the intoxicating flavours wafting up from the pot.

I hoped it wasn't chicken.